DATE			

Also by Jim Shepard

Love and Hydrogen: New and Selected Stories

Flights

Paper Doll

Lights Out in the Reptile House

Kiss of the Wolf

Nosferatu

Batting Against Castro: Stories

AS EDITOR

You've Got to Read This (with Ron Hansen)

Unleashed: Poems by Writers' Dogs (with Amy Hempel)

Writers at the Movies

PROJECT X

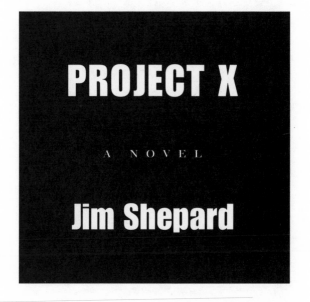

Alfred A. Knopf
New York
2004

THIS IS A BORZOI BOOK
PUBLISHED BY ALFRED A. KNOPF

Copyright © 2004 by Jim Shepard

www.aaknopf.com

Knopf, Borzoi Books, and the colophon are registered
trademarks of Random House, Inc.

Library of Congress Cataloging-in-Publication Data
Shepard, Jim.
Project X : a novel / Jim Shepard.—1st ed.
p. cm
ISBN 1-4000-4071-X (alk. paper)
1. Eighth grade (Education)—Fiction. 2. Male
friendship—Fiction. 3. School violence—Fiction.
4. Suburban life—Fiction. 5. Teenage boys—Fiction.
6. Revenge—Fiction.
I. Title.
PS3569.H39384P76 2003
813'.54—dc21   2003047575

Manufactured in the United States of America
First Edition

For Emmett and Aidan and Lucy

ACKNOWLEDGMENTS

The author wishes to acknowledge the following people, without whom this book would have been a paltrier thing, or no thing at all: Karen Shepard, Ron Hansen, and Geoff Sanborn; Gary Fisketjon and Amber Qureshi; and, though the events described herein are fictional, Priscilla Wolff, Tim Carlson, and the students at the Curtis School; Mary Alvord and the students in the Mount Greylock Regional School District; and all of the long-suffering teachers and students from Johnson Junior High and Stratford High School, from way back when.

PROJECT X

1

First day of FS and where are my good green pants? In the
wash. I have one pair of pants that aren't clown pants and
they're in the wash. They haven't been washed all summer but
today, this *morning,* they're in the wash. It's too cold for cargoes
and everything else in my drawer is Queer Nation, and sure
enough I'm the only one on the bus in shorts. "Scorcher, isn't
it?" a ninth-grader asks when he goes by my locker. I'm standing
there like I'm modeling beachwear. Kids across the hall chuckle
and point. I almost head home right then.

"FS, man," Flake says when he sees my face.

"I can't take it," I tell him. "It's like, twenty minutes, and I
can't take it."

"Look at your face," he says, and he has to laugh. He doesn't
mean it in a bad way.

I put my head on my hands in my locker and try to tear the
shelf off the wall.

"FS," he says. At least our first period classes are near each
other.

"FS," I tell him back. We don't even have homeroom together, though they told us over the summer we would. FS is fuckin' school. We argue over who thought of it.

My homeroom teacher has a big banner up on the bulletin board that says WELCOME TO EIGHTH GRADE! Underneath it there's a sign that says LEAVE NO CHILD UNSUCCESSFUL and a handout for EIGHT WAYS OF BEING SMART.

In the doorway of first-period English my feet like freeze. I can't even get into the room. *I will not fucking do this,* I think to myself. "What?" the English teacher says.

We're not in the same gym class, either. And his is fourth period and the first day stuff runs long, so there I am in the cafeteria without him. *C'mon, c'mon, c'mon,* I go to myself, like some god'll say, "Oh sorry, Hanratty, you want your only friend? I'll send him along."

And who's there: Hogan, Weensie, and all the other butt-wipes who are always after me. The kid from Darien we call Dickhead who beat me with a plank last spring. He pulled it from his tree house, and his friends held me down. Flake said when he saw my back that I was lucky there were no nails in it.

"Look who's watching his figure," the kid goes. I have like one milk pint on my tray.

"Eat me," I tell him. My eyes are tearing up and I want to pull them out and pound each of them flat on the tray.

"You're not sittin' on this side," the kid says.

"I'll sit where I want," I tell him. But I stand there and then head across the room away from him. I want to set fire to every single fixture and chair and window and crappy water-stained ceiling tile in this cafeteria. I can never eat anything here. Just taking a sip of water makes me want to hurl.

I'd fight if it was just him. But he's got eight thousand friends. Every asshole in the school is his friend.

I'm standing there with my tray. Pint of milk and a Rice

Krispies Treat in a little dish. Every table's worse than the one next to it. It's the worst feeling in the world.

When you're standing there in the middle of the floor with no one to eat with, there are about four kids who don't look at you. The cafeteria holds three hundred.

"Nice shorts," somebody says.

Even if you don't eat, you have to just stay until lunch is over anyway. There's a spot next to a kid from Latvia or Lithuania or something who smells. She has her hair moussed and smashed onto one side of her head like she fell asleep in tree sap. She showed up last year. She has fewer friends than Flake and me. And we only have each other.

"Is this seat taken?" I go.

"I yev a fren coming," she says.

I end up next to a girl who has to be the most beautiful person in her zip code. The rest of the table is all her friends. One of them I know from grammar school.

"This is a S.M.I.L.E. meeting," the one I know tells me. She shows me her folder: *Students Making an Impact Locally and Everywhere.* I eat my Rice Krispies Treat.

"We could sponsor a child," one girl goes.

"For a year?" somebody says.

"Well, what would *you* do?" the first girl goes. "Sponsor one for a week?"

They talk about a car wash. After a while they quiet down and I realize they're looking at me.

"You know who Kel Mitchell is?" the beautiful girl asks me.

"What?" I go. I switch my milk and Rice Krispies Treat on the tray. I never know what to do with my hands.

"You heard of Kel Mitchell?" she says.

When I keep looking at her, she says about me to her friends, "He's not a random guy."

"He's a random guy," one of them says. "He counts."

It's some kind of bet. "Yeah, I know who he is," I go. "He's the guy on that thing."

They're looking at me like they found a little lizard asleep on the table. "What thing?" one of them says.

"That thing," I go. My Krispies Treat's all sticky. I can't think of anything, but I'm not giving them the satisfaction. "You know, that thing on cable."

Their faces look like I may have hit it. The beautiful girl goes, "You are so bluffing."

"Mr. Hanratty," my fifth period social studies teacher says in front of the whole class. I haven't even sat down yet. "You going to be favoring us with more of your particular brand of sullenness this year?"

I write my name on the inside of the *20th Century Civilizations* cover: *E. Hanratty.*

"What are you shaking your head about?" he wants to know.

I'm not shaking my head about anything, I tell him.

He asks if I'm calling him a liar.

"I'm not calling you a liar," I tell him.

He says he'd like me to apologize to my classmates for wasting everybody's time at the beginning of the semester.

I apologize to them. Kids snicker. "Don't let it happen again," a kid behind me murmurs.

"We're going to be concentrating this year on Innovators," the teacher says. "Men and women of the twentieth century who found new ways of addressing society's problems." A kid in the last row makes a farting noise. The kids around him make snorty and strangled little sounds.

"Mahatma Gandhi, Martin Luther King," the teacher goes. "Mr. Hanratty? Any names to add to our list?"

"Richard Speck," I go.

So on day one I get detention. The secretary outside the vice principal's office congratulates me on being the first kid called in this year.

I don't see Flake for three straight periods.

"What's the matter with you?" a girl asks me on the stairs.

I have to call home when detention's over, since the buses all left an hour ago. My mother comes to get me and drives a mile and a half after I get in before she says anything. I measure it on the odometer.

"Your friend called four times," she says. "He didn't seem to know about your detention."

"You mad?" I ask.

"No, I'm proud," she says.

"Sorry," I tell her.

"So what'd you do?" she says. "Talk back?"

"Talk back," I tell her.

At dinner my dad tells me I'm grounded.

"No more malt shop for me," I go.

He tells me I'm grounded an extra week.

Flake can't believe it when I get him on the phone. "That's fucked up," he says. I can hear him sucking down a Go-Gurt. He goes through the things like he's five years old. "How could you get into trouble so fast with everybody?"

He likes what I told the teacher. He thinks my parents should've cut me some slack. "FS," he goes.

"FH," I tell him.

All the lights and the TV finally go off around midnight. My dad peeks in to make sure I'm not on the computer or sharpening a spoon to cut out his heart. "You asleep?" he says.

"Completely," I tell him. I have the covers over my face and a hand off each side of the bed.

"Try and avoid any felonies on day two," he says. "Though I know you already set a standard for yourself."

"I think Mom's waiting for you," I go.

"You got some mouth on you," he says.

"Good night," I tell him.

And I can't sleep. The digital clock on the nightstand makes loose little flipping noises when the minutes change. I put my underwear over it and then can't take it anymore and have to *see* how much time has passed. 1:14. 1:51. 1:54. 1:55. I lie there swearing like I'm calling Jesus Fucking Christ on my pillow radio. The flipping noises keep going, each one getting me closer to school.

I get up and go to the bathroom mirror. My nose is eight feet long and I've never had a haircut I liked. My glasses are crooked from always being broken. My lips are too big. If I get any skinnier I'll be able to pull a sock up to my neck.

"Somebody *help* me," I go. I squat on the floor with my hands behind my head and rock in place.

"You look worn out," my mom tells me at breakfast.

"Can I just have orange juice?" I go.

"I'm worried about your weight," she goes while she watches me drink it. My dad isn't even up yet. He's an econ professor at the college and his first class on Tuesdays isn't until two-something.

"Your pants are ready," she tells me, to cheer me up. "If you want to wear those green pants you were looking for."

At the bus stop I squat again. I pull my knapsack by the straps up to the top of my head. The two ninth-graders waiting with me look weirded out.

"That girl who's on everybody's shirts is like Satan," Flake goes at lunch. "She's like Evil Incarnate."

"You ever notice how many people around here wear green?" I ask him. "Everybody wears green."

"Yo," a seventh-grader says as he passes our table. Flake gives him a miniwave.

"What's *he* want?" I go.

Flake's looking at the dessert line. "I want like a million billion dollars just for travel," he says.

"Yo, faggot," a ninth-grader calls from a table across from us. When we look over he lobs something he's got wadded up. It's off by like six feet. Me and Flake make like we're looking for it way off in the distance. The kid wads up something else, but someone else whacks the back of his head with something and then they get into it.

Two girls from sixth-period art, Michelle and Tawanda, ask if they can sit with us.

"Free country," Flake goes.

They give him a look and turn to me. "So listen," Michelle says. When her jeans ride down, you can see the "*Victoria's Secret*" on the elastic band of her underwear. "We have to do this World of Color thing with three people."

"And?" Flake goes.

They look at him again. "Tawanda says you're really good," Michelle says to me. She's got ponytails that start way up on both sides of her head. "She says you're a really good artist."

"You're really good," Tawanda says.

She was in my art class in seventh grade. She did a self-portrait of a round face with big tears dripping out of the eyes called *Coffee Skin!* that the teacher went apeshit over. I did a drawing called *War the Scourge of Life* that had War swinging his mace through a whole city, with tiny bloody victims hanging off the spikes, and it got hung next to hers. After everybody's stuff was up she told me in the hall that my thing was amazing.

Flake starts doing his constipated-monkey thing. It's so impossible to describe: he grits his teeth with this sleepy expression and jiggles around in his seat and goes *Inka inka inka inka*. It kills us both. He's got thick brown hair and his ears stick out, so he makes a good monkey.

"What are you *doing*?" Michelle says.

"Inka inka inka inka," he goes.

"Yeah. Well," Tawanda says, "you want time to think about it? Want to tell us in class?"

"That'd be good," I tell them.

"He's not that funny," Michelle says.

"Inka inka inka inka," Flake tells her.

They both get up, holding their trays. "Don't forget," Michelle says.

"We want *you*," Tawanda says, pointing at me. "For our trio."

"We want *you*," Flake says after they've gone to sit at a table full of girls. All of them are talking and looking over at us. Michelle gives the back of her pants a tug.

"You da *man*," Flake says. "Tawanda wants to *touch* your art."

The whole table's still looking and laughing and Flake points at his crotch and then at them and then at his mouth. One of the girls nods and waves him over.

"Wouldja draw me a picture?" Flake asks me. Then he grits his teeth and acts sleepy. "Inka inka inka inka."

"So I was thinking," my mother says after school, standing in my room, on my clothes, waiting for me and Flake to stop what we're doing. She just walks in whether I've got the door shut or not. The lock doesn't work because I Jackie Chan-ed the knob a month ago when I was pissed and my dad said he wasn't going to fix it.

"Get off my clothes," I go.

"You don't want people walking on your clothes, get them off the floor," she tells me.

"Ouch," Flake goes. "Zinger, Dude."

"I don't need smart comments from you either, Roddy," she tells him, and Flake makes like he's zipping his lip.

She rubs her eyes with her fingertips. She takes her time doing it. Flake and I line up the fat girl in the plaid jumper and miss her but tip the frame, and the whole thing falls off the windowsill. Lately we've been aiming at my little brother's pre-school class pictures and seeing who we could hit from across the room with our potato guns. You dig the barrel into the potato before you shoot. We're always arguing about who hit what, but what's good is that the potato plug leaves a wet spot. So you can check.

"You're going to have little bits of potato everywhere," my mom says.

"This is really an outside kind of toy," Flake agrees. It's cracks like that that nearly get him thrown out of the house. One time my dad did throw him out.

"So you want to know *what* I was thinking?" my mom goes.

"The skinny kid with the glasses," Flake says. He digs his barrel into the potato and points.

"The one with the nose?" I go.

"No, the one with the—whaddaya mean?" Flake goes. "They all got noses."

"So go ahead," I tell him.

"Mr. Hanratty," my mom goes.

"You missed," I tell him.

"I know that," Flake says.

"I'm going to count to three," my mom goes.

"What?" I go. "What were you thinking?"

"I was thinking you guys might like to go out for that martial arts team or whatever that they're putting together," she goes. "Who's doing it, the soccer coach? It sounds right up your guys' alley."

"We don't have an alley," Flake goes.

"You guys could really use some extracurriculars," she goes.

"I know. We should be on the debate team," Flake goes.

"You'd be great," I tell him. "Whatever anybody said, you'd be like, 'Yeah? Your *mother*.'"

"What about you?" Flake goes. "Anytime anybody made a good point you'd be like—" He scrinches up his face like he's gonna cry.

"Shut up," I go.

My mom rubs her eyes again. When she stops, she looks sad. "Well, the thing they sent home is on the kitchen table," she finally says. "If you ever do decide you want to get out of this room."

She shuts the door and goes downstairs. I load up another round of potato and throw the gun into the closet.

"*College*," I finally go. "Anybody who goes to *college* . . ." I can't even finish the sentence.

"I wanna be president someday," Flake goes. "Or maybe Wizard Death Lord."

We *got* no Interests. We *got* no extracurriculars.

"I'm goin' to Fuck U," I tell him.

"We're goin' to Uzi State," he tells me back.

As opposed to our classmates. Our classmates achieve every minute of the day. They Strive Higher and Reach Farther. They put together model UN's while we sit around in study halls with our mouths open. They're captains of the mah-jongg JV or Vermont Junior Business Achievement or Hot Pants for Social Change. They think this shithole is something to be proud of. The ceilings are falling in and nobody's had new textbooks in a hundred years, but they're all School Spirit. They're dirps: Dicks in Responsible Positions. When one of them gives us grief for being such lazy shits, Flake'll lower his chin and go *Dirp*, like he's burping.

"Let's go throw rocks," Flake goes.

"Let's not and say we did," I tell him.

"So what do *you* want to do?" he goes. We don't watch TV. We hate TV. TV's a fucking blight.

We climb out the window onto the porch roof, jump over the breezeway to the garage, then hang off the gutter and drop down. Sometimes my mother thinks we're still up there in my room.

At the practice fields the JV boys' and girls' soccer teams are kicking balls around. They're almost all ninth-graders.

"What're we doing *here*?" I want to know.

"How about you stop complaining till *you* have an idea?" Flake says.

We decide to go to the fort we made under an off-ramp. You can only see in from one direction, and it's bigger than it looks. We found it one day playing a game where you ride through the gap in the guardrail at top speed. The gap's about two feet wide, and you have to bomb through without hooking a handlebar or elbow.

Somebody calls "Heads up!" and we duck and a soccer ball whonks Flake right on the head. The ball ends up in some wicked-looking prickers around a Dumpster.

I'm laughing. The kid who kicked the ball is laughing. He's still in his follow-through. Some of the girls' team is laughing.

"Ball?" the kid calls. He comes over to the chain-link fence and hangs on it, making faces at his friends.

Flake goes over to the Dumpster like he doesn't see the prickers and wades right in. "*Ow*," he says, and everybody laughs even more. He tears the ball out of the bush and looks at his hand.

"Who puts prickers around a fucking *Dumpster*?" he says. "What's *wrong* with this fucking town?"

"Hey ace, send it back," the kid goes.

Flake holds it out in front of him.

"Give it all you got, ace," another kid goes.

"I'll give it all I got," Flake says. I can see he's planning on kicking it to Peru, but he shanks it sideways down the street.

"Fuck," he shouts. I know better than to say anything.

"Nice *leg*," one of the kids says and starts to head around to the gate. The girls from the girls' team have turned away and gotten in a circle to do some kind of trapping exercise. Everyone's peppy and there's lots of shouted encouragement. It looks like the Dance of the Tards.

Flake and the kid reach the ball at the same time. Flake picks it up and turns and booms the thing it has to be fifty yards down the street. It bounces ten feet in the air and keeps going out into the intersection. Cars honk.

By the time I get there the kid's got Flake on his back and he's choking him with the collar of his own T-shirt. I grab the kid by the hair. Somebody punches me on the side of the head. We get piled on. The kid I grabbed hits me two or three times in the chest and shoulders as fast as he can and then grinds his hip on my face and someone kicks me in the back. Somebody else kicks me in the tailbone. Flake's screaming and swearing.

I'm twisting around like a fish. I'm hard to hold down. The kid on my head gets dumped off and another drops onto my chest with his knees on my arms. He knocks the wind out of me and slaps my face in various directions. Flake's on his stomach with a guy on his legs and a guy on his back. The guy on his back takes off one of his cleats and starts beating on Flake's head with it. The cleats are rubber. Flake's head pounds into the dirt. "I'm gonna *kill* you," Flake yells at him. "You're gonna *kill* me?" the kid repeats, and pounds him with the cleat. "I'm gonna kill you," Flake says. "You're gonna kill me?" the kid says.

"Let 'em *go*," one of the coaches hollers from the fence. "*Now.*"

Everybody piles off us, passing around congratulations.

Flake gives a kick from where he's lying but otherwise lets them go. I have my hands over my head. We hear them crossing the street.

There's grass and stuff in my hair. My nose and mouth are bloody. My ear's scraped up, too. My hand comes away from it wet. The blood's stringy and slimy from the crying. It's hard to spit. I don't want to move because of my tailbone. I shift my butt and that's enough to make me stop. Off in the distance I can hear the coach giving the kids shit.

"Fuck," is all we can say, a couple times, because everything hurts. Flake sniffles and writhes around.

"You all right?" I finally ask him. Over on the practice fields, the teams are heading in and the kids who kicked our ass are running laps.

"Fuck you," he says. I know how he feels: he wants the world to blow itself up, me included. He tips onto his back. His shirt looks like a slasher movie. His nose is a mess. There's dirt in his eyes. He puts some fingers on his face and feels around. He hasn't stopped crying yet.

"Aaaaaaaaaaaaaaaa," he says. It's not very loud. He tips back onto his side. It's one of the saddest sights I've seen all year.

"Aaaaauuaaaaauuaaah!" he screams. Even lying in the dirt, I jump a little. He wipes snot off his face and flings it. The kids running laps slow down to look over. Then they speed up again.

2

My mom sits next to me on the bed and helps with the ice. When the facecloth gets warm I pass it over and she dunks it in the bowl and wrings it out and hands it back. My lower lip's swollen and one eye's half-squinty. I look like Popeye throwing a tantrum.

"What's the matter with you?" she says in a soft voice. Like everybody else, she really wants to know. "Why can't you get along with the boys in your class?"

"They weren't *in* my class," I tell her. It's hard for her to hear through the facecloth.

"Is his nose broken?" Gus wants to know from the other side of the door. He's four and his favorite video's *The Making of Jaws* documentary.

"He's fine, Gus," my mom goes. "He just wants some time to himself."

"Can I see?" Gus asks.

"Then it wouldn't be time to himself," my mom tells him.

"*You're* in there," Gus goes.

"Why do you think you're always picking fights?" she asks me quietly.

"Are there guts?" Gus asks.

"No guts," my mom goes. "Are you watching the movie? 'Cause if you're not watching the movie I'll turn it off."

"I'm watchin' it," Gus tells her.

He's been on a *Predator* kick for a few weeks now. Flake thinks it's a scream. Flake brings him magazines like *Fangoria* and *Cinefantastique* with gross pictures of how they do the gore. He shows them to Gus when my mom isn't around. When Gus tells her about the *gushy* pictures Flake shows him, she says, "That's nice."

"I don't pick fights," I tell her.

"You just show up, and people hit you, right?" she asks.

I shrug. My eyes start to tear up because I'm feeling sorry for myself.

"So did you know any of these kids? They weren't in your grade?" she says.

"Ninth-graders hate us," I tell her.

"Why?" she asks.

"Well, eighth-graders hate us too," I go.

Gus opens the door and comes in and closes it behind him. "Can I come in?" he goes. He gets on the bed and lies on his side and only looks at me a little bit. It's something great he wants to save and not do all at once.

My dad comes home. We all just look at each other while he troops around downstairs. Then he comes up.

"What's this, a meeting?" he asks at the door.

"You don't look too surprised," I go. Meaning about my face.

"I'm not," he goes. He wears a shirt and tie and Levi's to class. He gets the Levi's at the Army-Navy store and spends like seventy-five dollars on the ties. "What happened to you?" he says.

"He was all bloody," Gus tells him.

"He got into a fight," my mom goes. She sounds like she's been carrying a big rock up a hill for a hundred years.

"His shirt was all bloody," Gus tells him.

"Some kids," I go.

He turns into his room, shaking his head. I hear the hangers in the closet.

"Is he all right?" he calls to my mom.

"He seems to be," she calls back.

"Was the Nightrider involved?" he wants to know.

He calls Flake the Nightrider because Flake's always wanting to go out when I'm supposed to be in for the night. One time I got caught climbing off the porch roof at three in the morning. I slipped and landed on our recycling bin for tin cans. Flake said we would've gotten caught by deaf people.

"Apparently they had a disagreement with most of the soccer team," my mom tells him.

"*High* school kids?" he says.

"JV," I go. He's still in his room, so I don't see if he has any reaction.

"I don't know what to do," my mom says, I guess to him. "Maybe another school."

"I'm not going to private school," I tell her. I got showed around one last year after I had so much trouble in sixth grade. They probably also figured it'd get me away from Flake. The kid assigned to be my special friend for the day let me sit on a meringue square somebody'd put on my seat in one of the classes. When I got home I put the flyer down the disposal and turned the disposal on. "So how'd it go?" my mom asked, when *she* got home.

Gus starts jumping on the bed. He has this game where he jumps on the bed and I cut his legs out from under him with my forearm.

I tell him to stop it. I have a big pillow under my tailbone, but the jumping doesn't help.

"Not now, honey," my mom says. "Your brother doesn't feel good."

"Is he hurt?" Gus asks, jumping.

"You're gonna be hurt, if you don't get down," my dad calls from the other room. "And are you watching that movie, or am I going to turn it off?"

Flake looks worse than I do.

"Look at you," I go when he comes over after supper.

"I'm gonna heal," he says. "You're always gonna look like that."

His dad cut his hair shorter so now his ears stick out even more. Plus he's got these cartoon eyebrows.

The only thing that cheers us up besides somebody getting hurt is mosh volleyball. It's the only sport we play. Flake doesn't like to call it a sport. We invented it ourselves. One of us serves off the roof of the garage and the other has to put it back up onto the roof without letting it hit the ground. The roof edge is low so you can sky and pin the thing to the top and then it just rolls off and is pretty much unreturnable. But what's great is, to slam it like that you have to throw yourself into the garage wall. The paint's all covered with scuff marks and our legs are all covered with bruises. My dad hates the game because it knocks stuff off the walls inside. Once we knocked the ladder onto his car.

You also can go up and block somebody's slam, which means both of you are hitting the wall at the same spot. On some serves, when the return bounces high, you can get way back and get a running start.

We go at it until it gets dark. I jam a finger and Flake gets grit from the roof shingles in his eye. I bang the shit out of my tailbone again and almost have to stop. I slam three in a row, and he starts leading with his knees when he goes up. He nails me in the balls and we have to take a break while I recover. I cut his legs out from under him on a block. "Asshole," he goes. "Fuckwad," I go back. "You are such an asshole," he goes. "You are such a fuckwad," I go back.

He wins 21–17. When we're heading in, the neighbor on that side of our yard calls from his kitchen window, "I'm sorry to see *that* game end."

A couple hours later on the way home Flake takes a dump on the guy's picnic table. He tells me about it in school the next day.

"How about this?" he goes. We're hanging around the school yard. Both our buses got there early, and we're not in a hurry to get inside. There's a jungle gym out in the middle of the field surrounded by a little fence because some kid almost got killed on it. "How about you went down the street with like an armored personnel carrier and blew in every other front door? Imagine how everybody'd *freak* trying to figure out what the deal was?"

"I don't think I wanna go to gym anymore," I tell him. "Think I could pretend to have parasites or something?"

We're pitching little rocks at each other's feet. We're pretty close to each other, but we haven't hit anything yet.

"Bethany what's her name is like everywhere lately, you notice that?" he goes.

"I never see her," I go.

"You never see her," he goes.

The first bell rings. They call it the first bell but it's a buzzer. "We better get in," I tell him.

He gives me that look. "You didn't see her. You didn't see her hanging out with Fischetti and those guys near the thing?"

"Yeah, I saw her *there*," I go.

"You saw her there," he goes.

"What do you, like her?" I ask. He's the one who brought it up.

"Suck my dog's chew toy, how's that?" he goes.

"Your mother's still busy with it," I tell him.

He doesn't answer for a minute. We're kind of hurrying because it's a long hallway. In big letters along the ceiling it says THE WALL OF RECOGNITION. There are all these framed photos of old teachers.

"Forgot my fucking *home*work," he says to himself. "God *damn* it," he goes when we're right outside his door.

"Bites," I go.

The second bell rings.

"Have a good day," I tell him. Then I catch my toe on the stair and almost kill myself. He leans his shoulder into the door to his room. "What're you, my mother?" he goes.

When I was little, one of the things I really loved was boating. Flake hadn't moved to town yet, but I really liked going with my parents. We had this six- or eight-foot sailboat that was seriously wide and dumpy, almost as wide as it was long. From the back it looked like a dog dish with a mast. My dad called it the Spirit Breaker, and when I asked him why he said it was a private joke. Every weekend in the summer we'd take it to the reservoir and toot around on it, all three of us jammed in. When you turned the rudder you hit somebody. When you were beaching and pulled out the centerboard, the other person in the front had to lean back.

One time we gave these other kids in a Sunfish a tow. They

broke some hardware at the top of their mast, so they were stuck over by the marshes, just drifting around and arguing. They didn't want to get out in the muck and walk the thing all the way around. My mom brought us about in a snappy little turn and my dad asked if they wanted a tow. There was a good wind. I remember being surprised he asked and surprised how happy it made me. What did I care? We had like eight hundred feet of rope in the bottom of the boat sloshing around in the water, for tying up to the dock. I got to be the guy who threw the rope when my mom brought us around again. And I held it while we pulled them along until my dad tied our end to the cleat in back. We got going pretty good. I remember the kid in front's face as we bounced through some waves the powerboats had left. He was older than I was but I still thought, *Good for you, kid,* like I was his dad. "That was really great," I remember telling my parents on the drive home. "It really was," I remember my mom agreeing.

"Mr. Pengue came by today," my mom goes.

"Okay," I go.

"He was surprisingly upset," my mom says.

We're all waiting for the pizza to heat up, and it's taking forever.

"Do you have it on defrost?" my dad asks. He's sitting at the table with his hands together on his plate.

My mom poses alongside the control panel like she's demonstrating it.

Gus is on his stomach under my chair with his hands around my ankle. He's squeezing and making hissing noises. One of his recent things is playing boa.

My mom pops the door and checks the pizza. It's a pile of four or five pieces, so she checks the middle. She thwaps the door shut again and loads in another thirty seconds. The pizza's two days old, so that may have something to do with it.

"Is there some other way to check it besides putting your thumb in it?" my dad asks.

"Not that I know of," she says.

Gus is still squeezing. "I can't breathe, I can't breathe," I tell him. He laughs. There's a tug when he bites my pant leg.

"So that was some story you told about Mr. Pengue," my dad says to my mom. The guy wants us to pronounce it "Pengway," but we say it like it's spelled. He's not a big favorite of ours.

"Yeah, so he came by," my mom goes. "Said he found the most interesting thing on his picnic table."

The bell dings on the microwave, and when she looks at me instead of doing something about it, I open it myself and pull out the pizza.

She's got a sitcom-mom look on, hand on her hip.

"It's ready," I go. Gus lets loose of my ankle and climbs out from under the chair. He hits his head on the table.

"You don't know anything about this?" she goes.

"I'm not an expert on pizza," I tell her.

"You know that's not what I mean," she says.

"Get me a beer?" my dad asks.

I stick the dish with the pizza on the table and go to the fridge.

"Listen to him sigh," he goes. "All he does is work to serve us." When I give him his beer and Gus his juice, he says, "So what's your mother talking about?"

My mom goes, "Tell your father what Mr. Pengue found on his picnic table."

"Oh, for Christ's sake," my dad says. "*You* tell me."

"I don't know what anybody found on their picnic table," I say.

"You don't," my mom goes.

"Oh my *God,*" my dad goes.

"I want him to say it," my mom explains.

"A severed head," I go. "A dying weasel. Four tickets to the Super Bowl."

"A pile of human—poop," she finally says.

My dad laughs.

"Encourage him," my mom goes.

"What do you, think *I* did it?" I go.

"You or your friend," she says.

"Because I didn't do anything," I go.

"Did you or did you not have some words with Mr. Pengue when you were playing out there?" she asks.

"We didn't have words with anybody," I go. Meanwhile the pizza's cold again.

"I don't need you all sullen. I'm asking you a question, is all," she says.

"It's cold again," my dad goes, dropping the pizza back onto the dish we warmed it up in, like that's the perfect end of a perfect day.

My mom stands up. She wasn't annoyed before, but she's getting there. "Give me your pizza, hon," she says to Gus. "I'll warm it up."

"It's warm," he says. He's still holding his head where he hit it.

"No it isn't." She puts her finger in it. "See?"

"There she goes again with the finger," my dad says.

"It's warm," Gus says. His other hand's got his sippy cup in his mouth, and he's talking around it.

"No it isn't," she says.

"I want noodles," he says.

"We're not having noodles," she says. "We're having pizza."

"Pizza?" he says.

"*Pizza,*" she says. "This. Right here. With the cheese and the sauce." She takes the dish over and slides it into the microwave. There's a big clatter. She cranks the thing.

"I think we're gonna have soup when *that's* finished," my dad says to me.

She looks at him like if she had a fork, she'd pin his hand to the table.

Gus is watching us, still sipping away.

"You take a dump on Pengue's table?" my dad asks. He doesn't seem amused.

"*No,*" I go.

"Your friend the Nightrider?"

"No," I go.

"Don't lie," my mom says.

"He may have," I go.

Gus's cup makes little noises.

"What do you *want* from me?" I finally go.

"Re*lax,*" my dad says, and Gus starts to cry.

"*Stop* it," my mom tells me. "What's the *matter* with you?"

My head feels like the main parts of it are blowing in different directions.

Gus wipes his eyes with the side of his sippy cup. He can stop crying like on a dime.

They're both just looking at me, because that's how it is: everything's my fault. If anything goes wrong anywhere, I'm to blame. Keep that in mind. My dad's giving me his I-may-be-a-cool-dad-but-that-doesn't-mean-I'm-a-pushover face. My mom's giving me her I-try-to-understand-can't-you-meet-me-halfway face. I have to book. I have to get out of there. I have to get out of my chair and up the stairs at a high rate of speed. At least I don't break anything on the way out. "Come *back* here!" my dad yells.

"What's the *matter* with him?" I hear my mom ask again,

scared. I slip taking the turn in the upstairs hallway and end up in my room on my hands and knees.

"He doesn't even like music," I hear her say, after a minute. "What kid his age doesn't like *music*?"

Gus says something. I get off my hands and knees.

"He's not mad," my dad tells him.

"Do you know *anybody* his age who doesn't like music?" my mom asks.

I can't hear what he answers.

I shut the door and get in bed with my clothes on. Now I'm sweating. I'm sweating through my pants. My body's all haywire. I pull the covers over my head. It's daylight out and I've got the covers over my head. What *is* wrong with me?

"You're fucked up," Flake says when I ask him. "You're fucked in the head. You're never gonna be normal."

"I'd settle for *para*normal," I go.

He laughs a little. "You think it's a joking matter," he goes.

We're in his room, the next day after school. His room's a box on the second floor. His dad let him paint one wall black, but only one. He's got a sticker on the window of a cartoon duck with no head and Magic Marker blood gushing out of the neck.

He's got something from his *Great Speeches of the Twentieth Century* boxed set going. It's the only thing we play.

"Put on the one with the guy who's always talking about the Reds," I tell him.

"I will if you tell me the guy's *name*," he says.

I throw his dresser knob at him. His furniture's always falling apart. There's a bottom desk drawer he hasn't opened in a year and a half. I didn't really wing the knob. "Ask Bethany," I go.

"You're not interested in anything constructive," he tells me. "You just sit around and piss your time away."

"You don't give a shit about anything," I tell him back. "You don't have the slightest regard for private property."

We're doing our parents.

"You shit in your nest," he goes. "And then the mess is supposed to be our problem."

We laugh. Sometimes he makes us both laugh.

"They're so worried about us but they do whatever they want," I go.

"I'm tired of talking about them," he goes.

"So let's talk about Bethany," I go.

"You are such a dildo," he goes. He says it like it surprises him every time.

"Let's talk about extracurriculars," I go. "So: you running for Student Government?" I go.

He laughs a little. He lies back and looks at the ceiling. There are marks up there from his throwing something. He bends his fingers until there are cracking noises and I can't look anymore. "So I had this idea," he goes.

Outside there's a banging noise. His dad's beating on something. He's a mediator for married couples who want to split up and a part-time hockey coach at the high school. He's always building something in his garage workshop and then getting pissed off when it comes out wrong.

Flake's pinching his eyelid like he found something strange there. He's still lying on his back but seems like he lost interest in what he was going to say. "Know how in cartoons," he finally says, "the coyote or whoever can run out over a cliff and hang there a second and realize what's going on before he falls?"

"Yeah?" I go when he doesn't say anything else.

"That's not that funny," he goes. "That can really happen."

We both think about that while his dad bangs away outside. There's the noise of tools being thrown onto the driveway outside the garage.

"So what's Grant up to?" I ask him. I call his dad by his first name, and for some reason this always pisses him off. This time it doesn't work.

"I feel like jerking off," he says, like it's like going away to a beautiful island.

"I'm not stopping you," I tell him. He makes a face.

"God *damn* it," his dad says outside. There's one more bang and a ringing sound.

"Whoops," Flake goes. "My hands smell like something," he goes. "Do your hands smell like anything?"

"So what was your idea?" I finally ask.

"I lifted some shit from Pen-gway's garage when I took that dump on his picnic table," he goes.

"Nice move, by the way, with the table," I complain.

"Why? You get in trouble?" He sounds interested.

"Course I got in trouble," I tell him. "What'd you think?" But it doesn't really bother me, and he knows it.

"I got this bug powder," he goes. "Roten-something. Supposed to be like supertoxic."

"So now I'm gonna get shit for *that,*" I go.

"You're not gonna get shit for anything, Mr. Fearless," he goes. "I took like a pound from a twenty-pound bag."

"What'd you carry it in?" I go.

"What do you give a shit?" he goes. "What're you, an environmentalist?"

"You'll probably get sick now," I go.

"That's right. I'll get sick now. Weenie," he says. "You want to hear this or not?"

"I want to hear this," I tell him.

"Roddy, get down here," his dad yells from the garage.

"What do you want?" Flake calls back. There's no answer.

"Roddy!" his dad finally yells.

"What do you *want*?" Flake yells back.

"I want you to get *down* here!" his dad yells.

Flake gets off the bed and stomps downstairs. I can't hear what they're arguing about once he gets to the garage.

I think about how there's always somebody worse off than

you are. A movie about a guy who's a brain in a jar: that guy's going, *Man, those guys who can't move their legs, they got it made.*

Flake comes stomping back upstairs.

"What'd your father want?" his mother calls from somewhere in the house.

"He wanted to put his dick inside me," he says, hauling himself up the banister.

"What?" his mom calls.

"He wanted to know where one of his tools was," he calls in a louder voice.

"You tell him?" his mom asks.

"I told him you had it," he says.

"What?" his mom says.

"I told him *you* had it," he yells.

"*I* don't have it," she says.

"I'm kidding," he says.

"What?" she says.

He shuts the door. "I'm here all alone," he goes. "It's like I'm living alone."

"So what's Grant building?" I ask him.

He ignores me.

"So what's your idea?" I go.

His idea is that we take this Roten-stuff and mix it with water and put it into the hot-air vents so it spreads around in the morning during homeroom.

"You want to be like those kids at that school?" I go. "In Colorado?"

"No," he says. "They were fuckups. I don't wanna be like anybody."

"How do we get it into the vents?" I go.

"I been doing some exploring in the basement down there," he goes.

"And how do we keep from getting sick?" I go.

We do it the day before, it turns out. We mix the stuff up in like a big saucepan and park that in the right spot, and when the furnace kicks on early the next morning, bingo.

"We have to buy a saucepan, so it can't be traced," he goes.

"Think people would really get sick?" I ask him.

Turns out he's more psyched about when they find the saucepan and everybody freaks. He's like, "The FBI, everybody, shit, the Navy *Seals*, everybody'll be crawling all over this place."

"People'll be like, 'Is this homegrown, or international?' " I go.

"Finally something'll *happen* in this fucking town," he goes. It's like he always says: natural disasters mean days off.

"Where is the stuff?" I go.

"I put it in the roof of Behan's doghouse," he goes.

"God. Suppose the dog like eats it or something?" I go, before I can stop myself.

"Gosh, I hope that doesn't happen," he goes. Behan's the German shepherd next door. He's on a chain and is always barking and jumping at Flake like he wants to tear his throat out. Flake gets in trouble for doing things like having picnics right outside the dog's reach.

"Is that the way it works?" I go. "You put it in water and it fizzes?"

"Yeah. It's Alka-Seltzer," he says.

"We have to know if it's gonna *work*," I tell him. He rolls his eyes like there's someone else in the room.

"I read the directions on the bag," he goes.

He takes out a few pieces of paper from his desk and starts sketching, like I went home. From the chair I can see an upside-down pot with curvy fumes coming off it and a number below: 200 *degrees*. He's not a very good artist.

"We have to get rid of stuff like that, too," I go. "That's just the kind of stuff somebody'll find."

He adds a long pipe going up to a big square of a room. He

adds a few more pipes. He folds the paper up, holds it up to show me, and then sticks it in my knapsack.

"That's gonna fall out when I take my books out, you know," I tell him.

On the next piece of paper he draws a stick figure inside a box with bars on it. The stick figure has its hands on the bars. He gives it a big nose and glasses.

"It looks like me, except it has no dick, so it must be you," I go.

Over its head he draws a big circle and then makes the circle a smiley face. He draws a word balloon next to it, and writes HI, FLAKE. WILL YOU ANSWER ALL MY QUESTIONS? inside. Then he takes the pencil in his fist and punches the point through the face over and over again.

"So when you wanna do it?" I go.

"The heat went on yesterday," he reminds me. It's true: in the morning it was cold, and you could smell the radiators in homeroom.

"I wish you could direct it at like specific rooms," I tell him.

He thinks about how cool that would be.

"This is just step one," he finally goes.

"Not even," I go.

"Do you have homework?" his mother calls from downstairs.

"I'm working on it," he calls back.

"With your friend in the room?" she wants to know.

"He's helping me," Flake explains.

"Is that kosher?" she asks.

Flake looks stumped. "I don't know," he finally calls. "What's 'kosher'?"

"Is that *okay*?" his mom calls.

"It's a group project," Flake calls.

"Why are we always shouting?" his mom calls. "Come to the top of the stairs."

He hauls himself off the bed, gritting his teeth. "I'm gonna use the stuff *here*," he says to himself. "Swear to God."

"*What*?" he says when he gets out in the hall.

"Don't yell at me like that," his mom warns him.

He bends over backward, holding on to the walls, and then straightens up again. "Can I help you?" he says, completely nice.

She lowers her voice. "Are you jerking me around again about this homework?"

"I am totally *not* jerking you around about it," he goes.

"Don't use that word," she tells him.

"*You* just used it," he goes.

It's quiet. I'm still in the chair, looking at the black wall over his bed. He doesn't have a single thing stuck up besides the headless duck on the window. For a while there was a picture from the newspaper of kids who'd died from a famine, but he tore it down.

"*What*?" Flake finally goes. "Ask Edwin. Edwin."

I get up and go out into the hall. They're both staring at each other.

"Edwin, do the two of you have a group project to work on?" his mom finally asks me.

"We sure do," I tell her.

We're both standing there, hands in our pockets, looking down at her. I know I'm gonna smile or something and blow it.

"What *is* your group project?" she asks me.

"Photosynthesis," I go.

Flake makes a snorty noise, too soft for her to hear.

She keeps looking at us, both of her hands on the banisters. "You guys are so smart." She taps a finger on the wood and walks away.

We go back to Flake's room and shut the door. He puts a finger against one nostril and blows boogers into his desk garbage can.

"We have to be totally careful," I tell him. "They can figure out who did it in so many ways now. They can use like DNA and stuff."

"DNA," he goes, like I've finally said the stupidest thing of all.

"What?" I go. "They *could*."

"Go like this," he tells me, then puts both hands over his mouth.

I do like he says.

He drops his hands. "Stay like that," he goes.

At ten o'clock the phone rings. My mom calls for me to pick it up.

"What's up," Flake says, then waits. "They off?"

"They're off," I go.

"Check," he says.

"They're off," I tell him.

"Just check," he goes.

I throw the phone across the room into the beanbag chair and troop downstairs. They're both watching television. I climb back up to my room.

"All right, Mr. Secret Spy," I go. "What do you want?"

"Tonight," he goes. "Three o'clock. Set your alarm."

"I don't think my alarm works," I go.

"Jesus Fucking Christ," he goes. He sighs. He hangs up.

Back downstairs, I ask my mom, "My alarm work?"

She looks up from the TV. "I'll get you up, honey," she goes. She turns back to the TV.

I climb back up to my room and fiddle with the thing. I set it for ten minutes ahead, then five minutes. I can't get it to work. It's a little plastic travel thing and I pound it flat a few times.

What difference does it make? I end up thinking. I'm not going to go to sleep anyhow.

Everybody's in a group. Everybody spends all their time thinking about their group. Or how they want to be in a different
group. It's a big shitpile with everybody shitting downward, so
you want to be high as possible. On top are the jocks, though
not all jocks. If you only do cross-country, you might as well be
on the chess team. Next to the jocks are kids they call the
Buffys, because they look like they came off TV. First day of seventh grade Flake and I were in homeroom and a girl said to him
about this new guy, "He is *so* Angel." The guy was good-looking
and had that shit in his hair. And Flake said back to her, "I have
no idea what you're talking about."

Behind the Buffys are the school-spirit types, the ones who
organize the Cookie Drives and Theme Dances and Adminis-
tration Appreciation Days. Behind them, the kids who play
music in a band. Behind them, the other jocks—the track
teams and the guys who swim the twelve-thousand-mile race
and stuff like that. Behind them, the artsy types. Behind
them, the kids that are good at something real, like math or
writing. Behind them, the theater kids. Behind them, the
rebels. Behind them, the druggies. Behind them, the kids
nobody notices. Behind them, the fuckups. Behind them, the
geeks. Behind them, the kids from like the sticks, the trailer types.
Behind them, the retards and kids with missing jaws and
shit. Behind them, us. Our group is a group of two.

Every so often people do nice things for each other but
mostly you don't trust anyone out of your group. That's just the
way things are.

They're all ants. Jock ants, artsy ants, theater ants.

Boil water and pour it down an anthill, the ants come out
another hole, Flake says.

My mom has a bad dream. I hear her downstairs. I go down
without making any noise and peek into their room. She's quiet

and then flops over and makes a whining noise. My dad sleeps through it. She makes the whining noise again.

It's just about three o'clock. I go back upstairs to get ready. I think about cutting holes in an old wool hat like a bank robber and then imagine Flake's face when he sees it. When he walks into the yard, he's wearing the saucepan on his head. I wave from the window and climb down.

The grass is wet and the crickets are going like it's summer. It feels great to be out. There's no moon I can see, so it's pretty dark. Flake sticks his arms out and takes a huge deep breath, then pounds on his chest like a gorilla. We walk over to his yard.

Behan sleeps in the neighbors' house. We check out the situation and everything's quiet. We walk over to the doghouse like we're all Whatever, but we're ready to run if we hear a noise. My feet are already soaked. When we get there Flake hands me the saucepan and crawls inside. His legs and butt don't fit in. I'm interested in the shingles on the little roof. You can pick off the pebbly stuff with your fingernails. He backs out with a Baggie in his hand and we take off.

"Nice watchdog," he says once we're out of the yard.

"Where'd you get the saucepan?" I ask. It doesn't look new.

Turns out he got it from the Goodwill bin.

"How do you think of shit like that?" I ask him.

He shrugs as he walks. We're moving pretty fast and keeping to the backyards. "I'm smarter than you," he goes.

He's smarter than me in some things, dumber in others.

Something's sloshing and I realize he's got a canteen on his belt under his sweatshirt. He sees me looking at it.

"Gotta have water," he says. "Wanna have to find a sink once we get in there?"

The school's a pretty good hike away, on foot. I don't know how long it takes to get there. At a red light we see a cop car, just hanging out.

When we finally get there I'm yawning like crazy.

"Now you got *me* doing it," Flake says. We're both pretty nervous.

My feet are tired. "How're we getting in?" I ask him.

"Watch," he says. He leads around to the old part of the building, to a window under the back stairs. It's totally dark under there and I can't see anything at all. I hold my hand out but can't even feel anything.

"Shit," Flake goes.

"What?" I go. "What's wrong?"

"I stuck a card in the window to hold it open," he goes. I can hear him feeling around. "Somebody must've found it."

"They *found* it?" I go. "So they know we're coming?"

"Yeah, it's a trap," Flake goes. "The whole thing's a trap." He ducks out from under the stairs and comes back a minute later. Glass breaks like somebody dropped a mug on the floor.

"You just broke the window?" I go.

"C'mon," he tells me. There are little brittle noises while he breaks away the broken pieces. "Watch the glass."

"They'll know that's how we got in," I tell him back. I can hear him already sliding through. I feel around the opening, then hop up on the ledge and slide one leg inside.

"You have to drop down a little," he says. "Hang on to the sill."

"Can we get out this way?" I go.

"Jeez, I sure hope so," he goes.

He knows where everything is, once we're in.

"You been down here before?" I ask him.

He takes out a little flashlight and starts shining it around in front of his feet. We come to three straight doors that turn out to be unlocked. Behind the last one I can see the little red pilot light of the furnace. I can feel the heat on that side of the room.

"Hold this," he says, handing me the flashlight. He squats and takes the saucepan and sets it on the floor and undoes his belt and slides out the canteen. I'm sweating and I'm not even doing anything. He pours the water into the saucepan and dumps the powder into the water. He reseals the Baggie and stuffs it into his pocket, then sloshes the pan a little to stir things around. He stands up.

There's a pin like the thing you stick in a turkey in the biggest pipe leading into the furnace, at the part where the pipe's going sideways. He slides the pin out and shifts the pipe around until it moves. It opens, but not far enough for the saucepan to fit in.

"*Shit,*" he says.

"It doesn't fit?" I go.

"*Shit,*" he says. He wrestles with it for five minutes, with me holding the light on it. Then he kicks the side of the furnace and sits on the floor.

"How about we pour some of it in the Baggie and just leave the Baggie open in there?" I ask him.

He doesn't say anything. He's probably wondering if you could get enough stuff in the Baggie to do any good.

"God *damn* it," he finally says.

The furnace clicks on. The open pipe makes it sound louder than it probably normally would.

"Lemme think," Flake goes. He stands up and walks over to the furnace. I zigzag the light around while he's thinking. "Shit," he goes. He slides the pipe back where it was, then drops his pants and pisses on the side of the furnace.

Walking home he's mad because his piss ended up splashing around and got on his shoes.

"What're you looking at?" he wants to know.

"Absolutely nothing," I go.

He squishes along. My feet are wetter than his, but his probably feel wetter. "Somebody's going to pay for this," he finally says.

"Your mom, when she washes your socks?" I go.

An old guy in an SUV trails us all the way home. He has to go about a mile an hour to keep from getting ahead of us. We stay on the road anyway. It's a long walk and the guy never speeds up. It must be four in the morning by this point. We don't see a single other car on the road. When we get to Flake's street, he turns to the SUV and puts his hands on both sides of his crotch and moves them up and down his thighs and belly. "Oh, *baby*," he says. "*C'mon*, baby." Then he turns and heads down to his house.

3

There's this sixth-grader who's decided he can't leave us alone. He always wears the same black t-shirt that says SCREW THE SYSTEM under whatever other shirt he's got on. Flake gets a kick out of it when he first sees it.

"Your mother lets you wear that?" he asks the kid. We're standing in the lunch line and the kid has six chocolate milks and nothing else on his tray.

"*Your* mother," the kid says back.

"He's not cracking on your mother," I tell him. "He's asking you a *question*."

"*Your* mother," the kid goes to me.

"Oh my God," Flake goes. "This little shit's crazier than I am."

You can see it's made the kid's day. "I'll kick your *ass*," the kid says. He's like three feet two. His hair sticks straight up.

Flake asks him his name.

"Herman," the kid says.

"Hermie," Flake says. "I like that."

"Herman," the kid says.

"Hermie," Flake says.

"Herman," the kid says.

"Well, I'm glad that's settled," I go.

"Up yours," the kid says.

Flake gives me a look. We both crack up.

"So can I sit with you?" the kid says, when we finally get through the line.

"No," Flake goes.

We have combination locks for our lockers. Every day I get worried I'm not going to be able to open it. That's what kind of hopeless feeboid pussy *I* am—I worry about being able to open my *locker*. The lock's no good. You have like two seconds to open it between classes, and everybody else is opening theirs. Three straight days I can't do it. The first day I try it twelve different ways, getting sweatier and sweatier, while everybody else gets their stuff and slams their doors and takes off. I stand there, looking at my little slip of paper like I can't read three numbers. During study period I ask for another locker. The janitor comes over to check it out, opens it no problem, and walks away. The second day I bang the thing around, kick it. Knee it. Some of the kids around me cheer. The third day I try to pretend I've already gotten what I need.

"Where's your text, young man?" my English teacher wants to know.

"In my locker," I tell her.

"What good is it doing you there?" she asks.

"Sometimes I wonder," I tell her.

"Did you hear me?" she goes. "What's it doing in your locker?"

I just sit there. The kid across from me holds up his book, to show me what it looks like.

"Why is it in your locker?" she goes.

The second hand makes its little jerks around the clock on the wall. Under the clock there's a construction-paper sign that says WHO OR WHOM???

"Do you want to explain why to the principal?" she asks me.

"He can't get his locker open," some kid finally says from the back of the room. Everybody laughs.

"Is that really true?" the teacher goes.

"Oh, fuck *me*," I say under my breath.

When I look up she's got the kind of expression you get when somebody drops something huge on your foot.

Nobody says anything for a minute. A boy in the back coughs. There's a plant on her desk, and a picture of Paris. You can tell because of the Eiffel Tower. There's a carved wood sign like businessmen have that stands up facing us. The sign says YES. AND . . . ?

I have a headache that goes from one ear to the other and over the top and down my neck. I wipe and wipe and wipe my eyes. "I guess you heard that, huh?" I finally go.

"Ms. Meier says you're not to come back to her room until you're ready to act like a human being," the vice principal tells me. He's a young guy and his jacket's too short for his arms. His shirtsleeves stick out like half a foot. I've got nothing against him.

I'm in his chair. He took the one that's supposed to be for the kids.

"When do you think that might be?" he wants to know.

I tilt my head and lift my shoulders.

"Can you use words?" he asks.

"I'm ready now," I tell him.

He leans forward and looks sideways, like the room goes on a long way in that direction. Then he looks back at me. "Anything you want to tell me?" he goes. "You having trouble at home?"

I think about it. "Yeah, I guess," I go.

"You want to talk to me about it?" he asks.

"I don't think so," I go.

He starts looking sideways again. He's got Extreme Sports photos like parasurfing and heliskiing over his bookcase. "I have to tell you, a lot of us are starting to worry about you," he tells me.

"A lot of us?" I go.

"Ms. Meier, myself, Mrs. Pruitt . . ." he goes. He makes it clear he could keep going. "So what happened today?" he asks.

"I can't get my locker open," I tell him.

The period bell rings and there's the usual thunder in the hall. Kids are yelling and laughing and locker doors are banging and crashing. No other kid in the school has a problem with his locker.

He's holding up his thumb and scraping away at the top of it. "You can't get your locker open," he finally says.

"Why does everyone repeat what I say?" I go.

"Is that what's supposed to've happened today?" he says.

"It's not *supposed* to've happened," I tell him. "It *did* happen. I couldn't get my locker open."

He keeps looking at me.

"I worry about it all the time. Getting up, getting on the bus, coming down the hall, I'm *worried*," I tell him. "I don't sleep, thinking about it."

"Why don't you get a new locker?" His voice is quiet, like I'm shitting him.

"The janitor wouldn't give me one," I tell him.

He puts his elbow on his knee and his chin in his hand.

"It's embarrassing," I tell him.

"Okay," he goes.

"Kids my age hate being embarrassed," I tell him.

The noise in the hall is pretty much gone by this point. Everybody's at their next class. He's got a framed list on the table next to me. It says, *Group Needs: Cooperation, Creativity, Sensitivity, Respect, Passion, Freedom of Speech, Change of Pace, Group Work, Clear Explanations, Fun.*

"Am I gonna get a note for next period?" I ask him.

He puts his fingers together under his nose like he's praying.

"Because I'm gonna need a note," I go.

He gets up from the kid's chair and comes around behind his desk. He picks up a framed picture of his dog. The frame has little plastic bones around the outside. All right, he finally says. Detention for a week. Starting today.

"I'm telling the *truth*, here," I go.

"Yeah. Our interview's over, Edwin," he goes.

"Whatever," I tell him.

"Tell your parents I'll be in touch," he goes.

My eyes feel like marbles they're so tired. I put my hands under my glasses and cover them up. My fingers feel cool on my eye sockets.

"You hear me?" he says.

"I may keep it a surprise," I go.

He laughs and shakes his head. "God," he says. "Kids like you used to get their butt kicked when I was a kid."

"They still do," I tell him.

There are four other kids in detention with me, two ninth-graders, and Tawanda, and another kid who always pulls his sweatshirt hood completely over his head and face. The monitor hasn't shown up yet.

"What're you doing here?" I go to Tawanda. The ninth-graders ignore us. One's cleaning his fingernails with a credit card. There's a photo on the wall of a kid staring into space. Underneath it says, THE MIND IS A TERRIBLE THING TO WASTE.

"You know," Tawanda goes. "Just bein' my old self."

The monitor comes in and gives us some rules and sits and starts doing his grade sheets. I pull out some homework. I'm the farthest back, near the window. The sweatshirt kid just sits there, a hood. One of the ninth-graders goes, "She took an entire grade off just for *that*?" There's a little scratching noise and when I look out Flake's doing his constipated monkey. I can't hear the *inka inka inka* through the glass. He makes a few signals that I can't figure out and then loses interest and leaves.

I'm behind on what I'm supposed to do for the World of Color project. There's paper and markers in my pack, so I could do that. I can't tell if Tawanda's working on it or not. She's too far up front. The idea sucks but it's our fault. Michelle wanted to do a poster of a rainforest tree with people of all different colors as fruit. Tawanda made a face and wanted to know if she meant heads hanging down like apples. They didn't have to hang like *apples*, Michelle told her. I asked if they could be severed heads. Michelle asked if we had any better ideas. Tawanda said she didn't. They both looked at me. "You tell me what to draw, I'll draw it," I told them. So we're supposed to be doing the apples.

We already started it. Some of the heads are already on the tree. My red Indian looks like Lava Man.

The ninth-grader in front of me tears the piece of paper he's been working on from his binder and passes it back. I'm so surprised that I take it and look at it. It says, "Asshole asshole asshole asshole asshole asshole asshole asshole asshole asshole asshole asshole asshole asshole asshole," all the way down the page. The whole thing is filled. "Asshole," he whispers.

"No talking," the monitor says.

"Asshole," the kid whispers again, after a minute.

"Mr. Hanratty," the monitor says. "What did I just say?"

"*I* didn't say anything," I go.

"Can I move my seat?" the ninth-grader asks.

"Leave him alone, Mr. Hanratty," the monitor says.

I've still got the sheet of *assholes* in my hand. It's a pretty amazing thing, when you think about it.

The ninth-grader raises his hand.

"What is it, Mr. Sfikas?" the monitor wants to know.

"He's swearing at me," the kid goes. "Can you tell him to stop?"

"He keeps putting his hand down his pants and grabbing himself," I go. "He keeps doing this thing with his hand."

The kid turns around with his mouth open.

"His whole chair moves," I go. "It's gross."

The other ninth-grader's laughing. Tawanda's turned all the way around in her chair. The kid gets a megadeath look on his face. "I'm gonna fucking *kill* you," he whispers. He says it like he can't really believe it himself.

"He's doing it again," I tell the monitor.

We get put into separate empty classrooms and told to not move. Mine has a big sign that says BLACK AND WHITE AND READ ALL OVER and has reviews of books by sixth-graders pinned up on the walls all around the room.

The monitor looks in every ten minutes or so. When he lets me out at four-thirty, the kid's waiting on the side steps with his friend. One of the custodians breaks it up. But before he gets there my shirt's torn off and one of my teeth gets knocked through my lip.

"So I know where that kid lives," Hermie tells me a couple days later between classes. He's wearing black-and-white camo pants. I didn't even know they made them that small.

"Can I help you?" I go. I'm wrestling with my combination lock. I'm in no mood for anything.

"Spin it all the way around three times before you start," he tells me.

I spin it once and then give it a yank. The whole locker shakes.

"Your mouth looks *all* fucked up," he says.

"Up yours, midget," I tell him. The hall's starting to thin out. The few lockers that are still open get shut.

My lower lip's so swollen that it feels like I could touch my nose with it. When I pass down the hall, kids look at it. The nice girls flinch and the mean ones talk about it.

"You are such a tube steak," he goes. He takes off to make it to his class. I make a caveman noise and bang my head against the locker and try it once more. It doesn't open. I leave my head against it. The bell rings. I spin the thing three times and try again, and it pops right open.

Before detention that afternoon he sticks his head into the detention room and gives me a little wave.

"You seen Freddy Budzinski?" he goes. His hair's a rat's nest on top but crew-cutty on the sides. It makes his neck look like a stick.

"You seen him or not?" he goes.

"What do you *want*?" I ask.

"I'll go slow," he tells me. "Have you seen Freddy Budzinski?"

"I have no idea who you're talking about," I tell him.

He looks around like he's thinking about buying the place, and then checks down the hall to see if the monitor's coming. "This your last day of detention?"

I take out my math book and flop it open.

"I'm gonna kill Freddy Budzinski when I see him," he goes.

"It's very hard to concentrate with all the noise in here," I tell him.

He flops in a chair next to me and sits still for a minute, spreading his legs as wide as he can. He starts drumming on the desktop with his thumbs.

"I really like that sound," I tell him. "Keep making that sound."

He stops and looks up at the history-project covers pinned on the walls. His mouth hangs open, and he breathes through it like something's clogged. On the floor there's a poster of a sunflower that somebody's torn down.

"So you don't want to know where that kid lives?" he finally goes.

I take off a sneaker and shake it out and fish around in it and put it back on. It takes a minute to tie it up again.

"Where you guys hanging out tonight?" he wants to know. Then he hears the monitor coming down the hall and he's out of his chair and over to the door in a second. "I'll come by and see what you guys're doing," he says. He bumps into the monitor trying to get through the door.

"This Student Council?" he asks.

"Does it *look* like Student Council?" the monitor asks.

"It really doesn't," Hermie goes. "I'm *all* turned around."

I can hear him getting running starts and sliding on the polished floor, all the way down the hall. The monitor's new today, taking over for the other guy. "What happened to *you*?" he wants to know when he sees my face.

Hermie comes by that night and bangs on the back-porch screen, but we don't let him in. Before he finally leaves he tells us where the ninth-grader lives. We spend the night coming up with things we could do to the kid but nothing any good. We walk over there the next night to see if anything better comes to us and run right into the kid and his friends and they chase us halfway home. One kid gets some great shots in on Flake's head before we get away, and someone else kicks me in the tailbone again, just when it was starting to feel better.

The next night we're all pissed off and depressed and sitting around in Flake's basement. "So you wanna check out my dad's guns?" he goes. His parents have gone out to a movie or dinner or Canada. They're not going to be back until late.

I'm sitting on the softest pillow in the house and have to keep getting up and moving it around underneath me. "What kind's he got?" I go. It's not like I've never seen a gun.

"Gun*s*," Flake goes. "More than one."

"Okay," I go. "What kind*s*?"

He starts upstairs. "Are you comin'?" he calls down, so I follow him. He's in his parents' bedroom. He pulls the shirts on hangers in his dad's closet to the side, and there's a box like a suitcase that could hold a little kid. Inside the box are some duffels, and inside the duffels are some guns.

We look at them on the bed. They're all heavy.

"This one's a carbine," he tells me. "It's from WW Two."

"*WW Two?*" I go. I can't get comfortable on my butt so end up on my hands and knees.

"Shut up," he says.

"And what's this?" I ask him.

"That's a Kalashnikov," he goes.

I get off the bed to pick it up, and swing it around with the butt on my shoulder, aiming at the ceiling. It feels like a parking meter.

"Russian," he says.

"Duh," I go.

"It's actually not," he goes. "It's Chinese. An AK-47. But the *K* stands for *Kalashnikov*. My dad says that's close enough for him."

It's big and ugly and black, with a stubby little barrel and a three-pronged sight.

The other one's called a nine-millimeter.

"So are these new?" I go.

"New hobby," he says. "He went to a gun show last week."

"Does he have bullets?" I go.

"He hides them in a different place," Flake goes.

The next night he calls when I'm brushing my teeth. My butt's still killing me. I think it might be broken. "You thinking what I'm thinking?" he asks.

"What're you thinking?" I ask. The mint in the toothpaste stings the scabs in my lip.

"I think you *are* thinking what I'm thinking," he goes.

I get sweaty for a minute and then it stops. "That *is* like those kids at that Colorado school," I tell him.

"Not the way we're gonna do it," he goes.

"What was that school called?" I go.

"What're you, the evening news?" he goes. "You want to do this or not?"

"I get to pick which one I use," I go.

"We'd go in with all three," he goes. "The other one'll be backup. And we gotta *plan* it, too. We gotta plan it better than that other thing."

"That's for sure," I go.

He's quiet for a minute. I go over to the sink and spit.

"What're you doing?" he wants to know.

"Brushing my teeth," I tell him.

"I'm not just talking here, you know," he goes. "I'm not just playing."

I spit again. "I didn't say you were."

"*You* just playing?" he goes.

"Nope," I tell him.

"I think you *are* just playing," he goes.

"Well," I go. "Wait and see."

The next day's Saturday and I'm up early. My sleep is all screwed up.

I'm lying in the middle of the parking lot at the grocery store. The parking lot's empty. The grocery store's closed.

"What're you doing down there?" somebody asks. He's a short little guy with a beret.

"Bonjour," I go.

"Hello to you, too," he says. "What're you doing down there?"

"Just resting," I tell him.

"Is it comfortable?" he asks.

"More or less," I go.

He's unloading stuff from his pickup. "You want a ride home?" he goes.

"I live right over here," I tell him.

He dumps a big case on the pavement and takes out a toolbox. More stuff is unpacked and snapped together. I turn my head so I can see, but I don't get up. It's a beautiful day. There was one cloud, but it left.

"Model rocketry," he goes. "Wanna see?"

"No," I tell him.

It takes forever to get set up. He hums to himself while he works. When he fires the first one off it makes a sound like a power nozzle on a hose and goes straight up until it's just a flicker and you're not even sure you can still see it. Then there's a pop, far off, and a dot appears: the parachute.

4

"Something's wrong with my tooth," he tells me while we're hanging from a tree. The branch we're on droops over a muck hole where a drainage pipe empties out. "When I press on it, it hurts like above my nose."

"I hate dentists," I go.

"Yeah," he goes.

He thinks about it, hanging and swinging.

"Look how much bigger my hand is than yours," he finally goes.

I climb up onto the branch and sit and look out over the weeds, happy.

"I can see it in the news afterwards," he goes. "The two murderous youths and their whatever plan—"

"Sinister," I tell him. "Sinister plan."

He doesn't say anything. Then he says, "My parents said I get twenty bucks for every A I get, and I haven't gotten an A yet."

"This is nice," I go. "It's nice when it's cold but not that cold."

"Let's get something to eat," he says. "You got money?"

At the convenience store we see Hermie down the Hostess Cake aisle. He's there with another kid as small as he is. "*You* got money," Flake says to him.

"I'm getting something for myself," he goes.

"Buy me something and you can hang around with us," Flake tells him.

"Take off," Hermie says to the other kid.

"Aw, *man*," the other kid says.

"You heard him," Flake tells him. The kid takes off.

Flake gets a burrito. I get some Slim Jims. Hermie gets Sugar Babies. We sit out on the curb eating and watching the idiots come and go.

"I found that kid Budzinski," Hermie goes.

"You kick his ass?" Flake asks. He's trying to get his mouth around an end of the burrito and the beans are sliding down his hand.

"Sorta," Hermie says.

"Sorta?" I go.

"He kicked mine," Hermie says.

"You look okay to me," I go. "What'd he use, a pillow?"

"He beat up a little kid like you?" Flake says. "People're fucked up."

"Fuck you," Hermie goes.

My dad's car pulls in and almost runs over our feet. My dad gets out. He stands there with his hands on his hips. He's got his jacket and tie on.

"Your dad's here," Flake goes.

My dad locks the car and walks over to us.

"Nice ride, Homey," Hermie tells him.

"Who's this?" my dad asks. He points at Hermie.

"Friend of ours," I tell him.

"He have a name?" he asks.

"Hermie," I go.

"Herman," Hermie says.

My dad heads into the convenience store, shaking his head. He must've just gotten out of class. We all watch him do his thing inside. When he comes out he's got a gallon of milk. "Now you're hanging around parking lots?" he asks me.

"Library's closed," Flake goes.

"Get in," my dad says. "I'll give you a ride home."

"I just ate," I go. I show him the Slim Jim wrapper behind me.

"Get in," he says.

"We get a ride, too?" Hermie wants to know.

"Say good-bye to the boys," my dad goes.

"So what've you two been up to?" my mom says at dinner. She's glopping out mashed potatoes onto everybody's dish.

"Nothing," I tell her. "Can I have more?"

"You're always planning something," she says.

I look at her. "Why'd you say that?" I go.

"I don't know," she says. "I hear you up there in your room, murmuring away. Planning on getting even with this guy or that guy."

"We're not planning on getting even with anybody," I go.

The bell rings and she gets up and takes the corn bread out of the oven and brings it to the table. We have to let it cool.

"Or doing your photosynthesis project," she goes. "Roddy's mother told me about that."

"It's a real project," I tell her.

"Well, I look forward to seeing it," she says.

We eat our dinner. Gus sings a song to himself.

"What've you learned so far?" she asks. "About photosynthesis?"

"Some strange shit," I go.

"Don't swear in front of your brother," she says.

"Sorry," I tell her.

"He can swear," Gus goes.

"No, he can't," my dad says.

"Can I swear?" Gus asks.

"No, you can't," my dad goes.

My mom's looking at me like we're sharing a secret. It weirds me out. She looks tired and worried.

"We got a nice call from the vice principal," my dad goes.

"Mom?" Gus goes.

"What'd he want?" I go.

"He wants us all to meet," my dad goes.

"Mom?" Gus goes.

"So we'll all meet," I go.

"I thought we talked about this," my dad goes. My mom remembers the corn bread and starts cutting it up and dishing it out.

"Mom?" Gus goes.

"You have a headache again?" my dad goes.

"Yeah," I tell him. I must've been rubbing my forehead.

"You've been getting a lot of those lately," my dad goes. "Maybe we'll have to have that looked at."

"Somebody should look at something," I go.

"Mom?" Gus goes.

"Yeah, honey?" my mom goes.

His little brain locks. You can see it. He smiles at having everybody's attention, and tilts his head to get the thought to roll from one end to the other. "Don't look at me," he goes.

"We're not looking at you," my dad tells him.

"Mom?" he goes.

"Yeah, honey?" my mom says. She really is a good mother.

"Do I have to go to school tomorrow?" he goes. He calls preschool school.

I'm sadder than usual for some reason. "Now what's the matter with *you*?" my dad says to me. It makes me jump.

"Do I just have like a sign on my face today?" I go.

"You have a glass head," my dad says.

"Remember when we used to tell you that when you were little?" my mom asks.

"I have a glass head," Gus goes.

"You sure do," my dad tells him.

I *do* remember when they used to tell me that, when I was little. I remember one Easter and a guy in a rabbit suit, but I don't know why. "So what am I thinking right now?" I ask them.

"What're you thinking right now," my dad says, giving it some thought. "You're thinking, 'Why don't they leave me alone?' " Gus takes a bite of mashed potatoes and holds his mouth open so I can see. "That's it, isn't it?" my dad goes.

"No," I go.

"That was it," he goes.

"What am I thinking now?" I go. I think: *Kalashnikov*.

"You're thinking, 'Why do I have to eat with them?' " my mom goes.

I laugh, and it cheers her up, but it makes me sadder than ever. Gus is still smiling. I'm pretty sure the world would be a better place if I was dead.

"Glass head," my mom goes.

"I don't know how you guys do it," I finally go.

"There're six doors in and out," Flake tells me. We're in our fort under the underpass. It's raining and the dirt smells wet. Every so often he ducks his head out to make sure nobody's around. "Four double doors and the two side doors near the fences."

"Six?" I go. That doesn't sound right.

"Yeah, six," he goes.

"Not eight?" I go.

"No," he goes. "Six. I counted." He goes back to drawing in the dirt.

"The two in the front," I go.

"Right, I counted those as one," he goes.

"Two in the back," I go. He stops talking and gives me his slit-eyed look. "Four the bus side," I go. "And then the two single doors."

"That's *six*," he goes, after I stop. He taps his stick on the drawing.

"I thought there were more," I go.

He looks at me the way he looks at kids who volunteer to be crossing guards.

"*Sorry*," I go.

"How do you even find the bus in the morning? Can I ask you that?" he goes.

"Like you never made a mistake," I go.

"You're a mistake," he goes.

"Your mother's a mistake," I go.

"God, I wish I could do this by myself," he goes.

"Why don'tcha?" I go.

We both shut up for a few minutes. It's raining harder and water is leaking in in little streams. I make a dam with my sneaker and keep one from getting to my butt.

Flake scratches the back of his head and looks at his drawing.

"So we try to seal up all the doors somehow?" I go.

"That's the problem," he goes. "We gotta get from there to there to there." He bounces his stick around the drawing. "We got to do it pretty fast, and we got to do it so they can't be opened that fast."

We both look at the outline in the dirt: a big box of an L with little slashes for the doors.

"We could split up," I go.

"Yeah, well, even then," he goes.

We get discouraged, sitting there. Flake shifts around and stares at the thing with his arms on his knees and his fists on both sides of his face.

"Where's the gym?" I go.

"Over here," he goes. He leaves the stick on it. He yawns. It makes me yawn. He farts. I make a face and he waves his arm to move the air. "What do you care where the gym is?" he goes.

"The gym only has two sets of double doors and that little door," I tell him.

He's still got his fists on his face. His head starts moving, up and down. "During assembly," he goes.

"Maybe we could do something with the little door ahead of time," I go.

He keeps nodding, looking at the dirt.

"Break the lock or something," I go.

"Right before," he goes. "Then you come in this double door." He puts his finger in the dirt. "And I come in this one." He's still nodding, picturing the whole thing. He looks at me, happy for the first time all day. "This is a good idea," he goes. "This is a good idea, Edwin."

"What'd you teach today?" I ask my dad. Dinner's late because the sweet potatoes are taking forever. He and Gus are hanging out on his bed watching TV. He's lying on his back with his head on the headboard, and Gus is sitting on his chest. He has to tilt his head to the side to see.

"Wanna see my wicked face?" Gus asks. When I tell him sure, he pulls his lower eyelids down and grimaces.

"Macro," my dad goes.

"Was it fun?" I ask him.

"I like macro," he says, then looks at me sideways. "You looking for something?"

I wander into the kitchen.

"What's everybody up to?" my mom wants to know.

They're watching TV, I tell her. She's cutting up an avocado for a salad.

"Are there any other kids at school who don't watch TV?" she asks.

"Besides me, you mean," I go.

"Besides you and Roddy," she says.

"Not that I know of," I tell her.

"Don't kids talk about shows and stuff that're on all the time?" she asks.

"All the time," I go.

"Don't you feel left out?" she asks.

"All the time," I go.

She washes her hands and dries them and checks the sweet potatoes in the oven. They must be done because she sticks each of them with a fork and then pulls them out and dumps them in a bowl.

"I think Gus is going to turn out to be normal," I go.

"Oh, Edwin," she says. She acts like the potato bowl is too heavy to lift. "Don't say that."

"He is," I tell her.

"You're not abnormal," she says.

"I'm not?" I go.

She starts putting stuff on the table.

"I'm not?" I go.

"Look, I don't have the energy to fight about this right now," she goes.

"I'm not fighting," I go. "I'm asking a question."

"What's the question?" she asks, sitting down alone at the dining room table.

"I'm not abnormal?" I go.

"Let's *move*," she calls to everybody else. "Dinner!"

I sit and take a sweet potato and cut it open. It's like lava inside. "I'm glad to know I'm not abnormal," I go.

"Edwin, please," she goes.

"Edwin please what?" my dad goes. He's in charge of drinks, so he hits the fridge and brings over a pitcher of ice water for them and a carton of milk for us.

"Turns out I'm not abnormal," I go.

"Well, let's not rush to judgment on *that* one," he goes.

"Honey," my mom goes.

"What?" he goes. "I can't kid around with him?"

She shakes her head and starts dishing out the meat.

"You're fine," my dad says to me. "I grew up with kids who make you and Flake look like Archie and Jughead."

Everybody eats for a while. I'm mad I got into this.

"I got a rash on my butt," Gus says.

"Does it still hurt?" my mom asks.

"Wanna see?" Gus says to me.

"Maybe later," I go.

He gets up on his chair and drops his drawers. The rash doesn't look so good.

"Whoa," I go. It's just what he wanted to hear.

"You remember when I was six and there was that huge birthday party, pool party?" I ask my mom and dad. "And I didn't want to go?"

Gus pulls up his pants and sits back down. "We remember," my mom says.

"How come you made me go to that?" I ask.

"You told that little boy you were going to go at least a dozen times," my mom says. "Remember how he kept calling to make sure you were still coming?"

"I really didn't want to go," I tell them. "I *really* didn't want to go."

"Well, maybe we shouldn't've made you go," my dad says.

The kid's older brothers had all their friends there. They took my bathing suit. They locked me in the pool shed. When I got out I had to run around trying to get my suit back, covering myself with a Frisbee. Two kids took my picture.

"Poor Edwin had a hard time today," the kid's mother told my mom when she came to pick me up. I got a shovel from our garage and tried to go back. My mom had to call my dad.

"No more pool parties," my dad goes.

"You better believe it," I tell him.

"All right, we made a mistake," he tells me. "From now on, whatever happens, it's because we made that one mistake."

"Can we just drop this?" my mom goes.

Gus is taking all this in without saying a thing.

"*I* don't need to talk about it," I tell her.

The phone rings. Nobody answers it. The answering machine clicks on but whoever it is doesn't leave a message.

"You just shouldn't have made me go, that's all," I tell her.

"Oh my God," my mom says.

5

My English teacher is coming down the hall in the morning before homeroom. Of course I'm having trouble with my locker and when I finally rip it open I'm rushing to dump stuff out of my knapsack and pick up other stuff for first and second period. My math book and some papers flop onto the floor, and Dickhead, the kid who beat me with a plank, is going by and scuffs them out into the middle of the hall.

Of course my teacher doesn't see that. She helps me pick stuff up.

"Thanks, Ms. Meier," I tell her.

"What's this?" she goes. It's a drawing of a pot with curvy fumes coming off it. The pot has a skull and crossbones on it and next to the pot it says *200 degrees* in Flake's spaz handwriting.

The look on my face catches her attention. I'm staring at the thing thinking, *I can't believe I didn't get rid of this.*

"What is this?" she goes.

It's a chemistry experiment, I tell her. The bell rings.

"You're not old enough to take chemistry," she says.

"No, I don't mean for school," I go. "My dad got me one of those sets."

She turns the paper over to look at the front again and asks, "What's supposed to be in the pot?"

"I don't know," I tell her. "Chemicals."

"Why does it have a skull and crossbones?" she wants to know.

"I don't know. Because it looks cool," I tell her.

She thinks about it for a while and then hands it back to me.

"Can you write me a pass?" I ask her.

She says okay and before homeroom I go to the bathroom. There's a boy leaning over the sink to put on Chap-Stick in the bathroom mirror. In a stall I tear the picture into two thousand pieces and flush them down the toilet.

"Bowel trouble?" the vice principal asks when I pop out into the hall. It's empty and quiet.

"I got diarrhea," I tell him.

"Mr. Davis, do you think I have problems?" Bethany asks as she goes by with a girlfriend.

"I reserve the right to not answer that question," he tells her, and they both laugh.

"Mighty quiet in there for diarrhea," he tells me once they're gone.

Up yours, I think, on the way to homeroom.

Step two is figuring out a way of sealing up the little door in the gym. We talk about it either at Flake's house or in the fort. After what my mom said about our sitting around and talking about getting even with people, my room's out.

Step one I get all the credit for, according to Flake. Step one was figuring out we could do it in the gym instead of having to lock up the whole school.

The door's not very big but it's a harder problem than it looks like. It has to be something we can do fast. It has to be something we can do with stuff we can bring to school without anybody noticing. And it has to be something nobody'd notice for at least a few minutes.

We're not coming up with anything right off the top of our heads.

We've already figured other stuff out. We'd have the guns in our lockers. We'd go for the all-school assembly before Thanksgiving. They hang big crepe-paper turkeys and shit on the windows and doors, and that might help hide whatever we do to the lock.

I keep coming back to duct tape, because it's one of those doors where you hit the bar to open it from the inside. But Flake thinks duct tape's too easy to see and wouldn't be strong enough anyway.

"With enough tape it would be strong enough," I go. We're in his bedroom and he's got the *Great Speeches* CD going in case his mother or somebody wanders by the door.

"What're you, gonna stand there for thirty minutes wrapping duct tape around things?" he goes.

"I don't think it would take that long," I tell him.

"Who do you think was the best serial killer?" he goes. He knows I have a book about it.

"It depends," I go. "Ed Gein was pretty fucked up."

He looks grossed out. I told him about Ed Gein.

"I keep thinking we could get a hammer or chisel and just smash the shit out of the thing that goes into the wall," he goes. "You know, the thing that sticks out."

"Yeah, like that wouldn't make a gigantic noise," I go.

"Well, I'd rather make a gigantic noise than stand there for eight hours," he goes. "If nobody sees you right when you do it, you could take off by the time people came."

Suppose they came and checked out the door, I ask, and he

makes a face. What about we *bring* a lock, I ask. Like a bike lock.

"There's nothing on the wall to lock the bar to," he says.

We think about it. He's got a sketch of the door and draws lines from the bar in various directions. "What we need to do is do like a test," he goes.

He's right. That's the only way we're going to figure this out. "We can't be all set to go and get there and find out it's not gonna work," I tell him.

"Who's got doors like that that we can screw around with?" he wants to know.

"The mall," I go.

"No, those are different," he goes. "Besides, who's gonna let us screw around with doors at the mall?"

I keep thinking.

"Use your head," he goes.

"Use yours," I tell him.

We sit there, Flake drawing big *X*'s on his sketch pad.

"Who's this?" I ask him, about who's talking on the CD.

"Charles Lindbergh," he goes. "Some of those doors in the basement near the furnace were the bar kind."

"We're gonna go back *there*?" I go. "We broke the window. They know someone was there."

"We'll check it out," he says. "We'll wait a few weeks. If it doesn't look easy, we won't do it."

"I don't know," I go.

"Well, then come up with someplace else," he says, like it's settled.

I don't like it but it's the best plan we've got right now. "What'd Charles Lindbergh do?" I go.

"Why don't you read a book and find out?" he goes.

"I just told you about Ed Gein," I go.

"Ever hear of the *Spirit of St. Louis*?" he goes.

"Yeah," I go.

"So there you go," he says.

"So I don't like sports," I go.

"God, help me," he goes. "Mother of God, help me."

"Oh, yeah. Poor you," I go.

When his dad drives off to pick up some takeout we head into the garage to investigate his tools.

We start with his big red toolbox. He keeps it locked, but even I've seen where he hides the key. We root around in it. Everything's big and heavy, so digging around makes an unbelievable amount of noise.

"What're you boys doing out there?" his mom calls from the kitchen window.

"Making trouble," Flake calls back.

"You better not be in your father's things," she calls.

He stops rooting for minute, to let her wander into another room.

"What is *this*?" I ask. I hold it up.

"I have no clue," he goes. "Put it back."

There's nothing it looks like we can use. Needle-nose pliers, regular pliers, a big red wrench I can barely lift, two hammers, two measuring tapes. Little plastic boxes of screws. Rubber gloves.

He grinds his teeth like he does when he's starting to get pissed. I barely get my fingers out of there before he slams the top shut.

"What about up here?" I point at the particleboard his dad hung on the wall. It has holes for hooks and big stuff hanging from the hooks. Oversized scissors, a T square, an old hand drill, electrical tape, duct tape. Bungee cords. I take one down. "What about this?" I go.

"How long's it take to take off bungee cords?" he goes. He makes a disgusted noise that sounds like a push on a bicycle pump. "How about Scotch tape?" he goes.

"Okay. It was just a *question*," I go.

"You could slide like a rake handle across the door and through the bar," I tell him a minute later.

"I thought of that," he tells me. "You can also just slide it right back out again."

"Yeah," I go.

He sits on the cement, checking for wet spots from oil or antifreeze or whatever else is leaking out of his father's car. I squat next to him.

"Worried about your pants?" he goes.

"I got like one nonqueer pair of pants," I go. "I'm not getting shit all over them for no reason."

"What's up with that?" he goes. "Why can't you buy another pair a pants?"

"Roddy?" his mom calls. It sounds like she's farther away than the kitchen.

"Right here," Flake calls back.

We look up at the particleboard and all around the rest of the garage.

"I was always jealous of kids who could take like two sticks and build something that would catch a raccoon," he goes.

I know how he feels. "It sucks that we can't think of anything," I tell him. It really does.

"All we're trying to do is keep a lot of people in one place while we shoot at them," he goes. "Why's it have to be so hard?"

His dad's car pulls into the driveway. He accelerates when he sees Flake sitting in the middle of his garage and then he brakes before he reaches us.

"Suppose your brakes didn't work?" Flake goes when his dad gets out of the car.

His dad hefts the takeout bag onto his shoulder like he's starting a long hike. "My point entirely," he goes.

"What's that mean?" I ask once his dad's in the house.

"Who knows, with him?" Flake goes. He gets off the floor and wipes his hands.

It's a nice day so his dad and mom come back outside with the takeout and a half-gallon of ginger ale and some plastic cups. They spread out on the picnic table. They don't ask if we want anything, so we sit in the grass and look over at them. Flake chews on individual blades and then a dandelion stalk. The sun feels good on my back.

"Your parents ever try and get you interested in sports?" his dad calls over to me.

I shrug.

He shakes his head. It looks like they're having quesadillas. "Music?" he asks.

My mom got me an acoustic guitar one year for Christmas. Gus used to fill it with dirt and drag it around the yard on a string. "Nah," I go.

"We tried to get Roddy excited about music," his dad goes.

"You got me one of those pianos for like one-year-olds," Flake goes.

"You want a real piano?" his mom asks.

"No," Flake goes.

"We'll get you a real piano if you want one," his mom says.

"I don't want one," he goes.

"All right, then," his dad says.

"*God,*" Flake goes, under his breath.

"Roddy's grandmother was a wonderful musician," his dad goes.

Flake's looking off into the neighbor's yard.

"Was she?" I finally go.

"She could've been a professional," his dad goes.

"All she ever did was complain about her health," Flake goes to me. "And she lived to be like a hundred and two."

"What'd he say?" his dad goes.

"What do you care?" Flake goes.

"What'd you *say* to him?" his dad goes.

"He was telling me about her," I go.

He looks skeptical but keeps eating. Flake's mom is off in her own world, looking at her ginger ale.

"How did I end up with a kid with no ambition?" his dad finally goes. His mom shakes her head, like *she* doesn't know.

"Don't worry about the no ambition part," Flake tells him.

"You got some?" his dad asks.

"I'm working on it," Flake goes.

"You don't look like you're working on it," his dad says.

"I'm working on it right now," Flake goes.

I whack his leg to shut him up. He tears up more grass and won't look at me.

His dad spreads out the quesadilla's wrapping with the palm of his hand. "Glad to hear it," he finally goes.

6

I come over to Flake's the next day after school and he's in his garage sitting on the floor doing something with his hand. He doesn't answer when I say hey from the driveway.

I ask what he's doing. Coming in out of the sunlight it's hard to see at first. He's holding a can of spray paint an inch from the back of his hand and spraying the same spot. The paint's blue. It's dripping onto the cement under his hand.

"What're you *doing*?" I go.

He keeps spraying. The smell's making his eyes water.

"What're you *doing*?" I go.

He stops and looks at the spot he's been spraying.

"Your dad's gonna be pissed about the paint on the floor," I tell him.

He looks at it. It's not a very big puddle, but still.

"A few years ago I was trying to make a model," he tells me. He's got his eye right up to the part of his hand where the paint is. "When I was spray painting it, I found something out."

"So?" I finally go. "What'd you find out?"

He puts the nozzle up against the part he's already painted on his hand and sprays again. "You can fuck up your skin like this," he goes. "If you do it long enough."

I crouch next to him. Like that'll help me figure out what he thinks he's doing. Up close, the smell from the paint's so intense that I feel like I'm squinting when I'm not.

"You are one weird kid," I finally go.

"It's like a burn, but a burn that doesn't burn," he goes.

"See?" he goes. "It's making a blister."

"What'd you do to your hand, Roddy?" my mom asks as soon as we come into the house.

"Burned it," Flake goes.

"How'd you burn it?" my mom goes. She's all alarmed. She gets in front of us.

"Wasn't careful," he goes.

"Were you playing with matches?" she asks. She looks at me.

"Oh, no," he goes.

"Let me see," she goes. She takes his hand with both of hers. He cleaned the paint off with thinner and that made the blistering worse. There are pink bubbles from his thumb to his pointer finger and down to his wrist.

"I got aloe," she goes. "You want aloe?"

"My mom gave me some," he goes.

"Well, I hope you weren't doing something stupid," she goes.

"Sometimes I need to be more careful," he tells her. He means it.

"Were you guys doing anything stupid?" she asks me.

"He was already hurt when I got there," I go. "I just brought him over here."

We're up in my room a minute and a half before the phone rings and my mom calls up the stairs that it's for Flake.

"Were you painting in my garage?" his dad asks him. I can hear every word he says.

"We tried to clean it up," Flake says.

"You didn't try too hard," his dad goes.

"I can hear like every word he's saying," I tell Flake.

He nods. "I'll clean it some more," he promises.

His dad swears a few times and then gets off the phone.

We sit and stare at his hand for a while. "Edwin," my mom calls.

"Edwin," Flake goes.

I go over to the door and open it. "What do you want?" I call down to her.

"There's a boy here to see you," she goes.

I look over at Flake, who thinks it's funny.

"I don't know any boys," I go.

"I'm sending him up," she says.

Hermie comes up the stairs two at a time.

"Who said you could come over?" I go.

"Your mom," he goes.

"My mom said you could come *up*," I tell him. "Who said you could come *over*?"

"*I* said," he goes.

"*You* said?" Flake goes. "Midgets make the rules now?"

"Don't make me kick your ass," Hermie goes. He's having the time of his tiny life. "Listen," he goes. He's looking around the room.

"Don't get comfortable," I tell him.

"I got a proposition for you guys," he goes.

"A proposition?" Flake says.

"Yeah, a proposition," Hermie goes. "You wanna hear it or not?"

Flake grabs him by the shorts and the collar of his shirt. I can hear Hermie grabbing at the banister as they go downstairs and complaining about something all the way out. The back door slams, then Flake comes walking back up and shuts the door behind him.

"Did that boy leave already?" my mom calls from the back of the house.

We can't talk in my house and Flake doesn't want to go back to his so we walk to the fort. When we get up to the underpass and duck under the concrete Flake hits his head. He's still swearing when we see Dickhead and Weensie and two other kids sitting there with our candles and sketch pads. We had a box stuck up on a drainage pipe with some stuff in it, and the stuff is spread all over the dirt. There's nothing on any of the sketch pads that anybody could figure out.

"This is ours," Flake goes, holding his head.

"Yours?" Weensie goes. "You own the highway?" I don't know where he got his name. He's got freckles that look like they were drawn on and a space between his front teeth.

"Oh, this is *theirs*," one of the other kids says. "Everything here is theirs."

The other kids laugh.

"That's ours too," Flake says, about the sketch pads and candles.

"Why don't you take 'em from us?" Dickhead says.

We stand there, half in and half out. *"Fuck,"* Flake finally says. He rubs his head some more.

"Hurt yourself?" Dickhead goes.

"You dumped all our shit out," I go. "Who said you could dump all our shit out?" We had gum, pencils, a little flashlight and some napkins in the box. Flake liked to jerk off sometimes.

They don't say anything. They just look at us. Dickhead has one droopy eye, and he's always grinning up at you, like you're just about to get the joke.

"Gimme the flashlight," I go. "And gimme the sketch pads."

"Oooo," Weensie and another kid go. "Oooo."

Weensie turns the flashlight on and shines it in my eyes. He turns it off and on again. He shakes his hand to make it like a strobe.

"Give him the flashlight," Flake goes. He's finally let go of his head.

They make more scared noises. Flake wanders off and circles around on the slope up to the road. When he comes back he's got a flat rock the size of a paperback.

"What're you, gonna *hit* us with that?" Dickhead goes. "You tryin' to fucking scare me with a *rock*?"

Flake takes the flat side and brings it to his head, and then lowers it and brings it back up again, like he's demonstrating how to do something.

"What the fuck is wrong with you?" Dickhead goes. He sounds like he really wants to know, all of a sudden.

No one says anything. One of the kids coughs and clears his throat and spits. "Aw, give it to him," another kid says.

"Why should I?" Weensie asks him. But then he rolls the flashlight over to me.

"Give him the sketch pads," Flake goes.

"Put the rock down," Dickhead goes.

"Give him the sketch pads," Flake goes.

"You put the rock down," Dickhead goes.

Flake puts the rock at his feet.

"These drawings suck, by the way," Dickhead goes. He tosses the two little pads out to me.

"Blow me," Flake goes.

"I'll fucking kick your ass," Dickhead goes.

"Kick my ass," Flake goes.

You can see Dickhead deciding.

"Kick my ass," Flake goes.

Dickhead starts to get up.

"Let 'em go," Weensie says.

"Who wants to screw around with these dildoes?" another kid says.

"This is our place," Dickhead says to Flake. "You find another place to blow each other. And take your rocks with you."

"Oooo," one of the kids goes. The rest of them laugh.

Flake turns and is halfway up the embankment before I realize he's leaving. We don't talk at all on the walk home. When he turns off for his house, he doesn't say anything and neither do I.

"You still pissed?" I ask him the next day, which is a Saturday. His dad and mom are spending the afternoon getting shown around a condo they're not going to buy so they can get a free TV. Flake's pulled out the guns and ammo and we're making sure we know how everything fits together.

"*You still pissed?*" he goes, in a pussy voice.

I tilt up the carbine's barrel. "Put this in your mouth," I go.

He's got newspaper spread on his dad's bed so we don't get oil on the blanket. The Kalashnikov's easy. You can see right where the clip goes. At first I don't want to put it in because I'm worried we won't be able to get it out.

"We're gonna have to get it out at *school*," he says.

"We are?" I go.

"What happens when you want to change clips?" he wants to know.

"Oh, yeah," I go.

He shakes his head.

I turn over his dad's nine-millimeter, which looks like something a secret agent would use. Its clip is heavier than a rock that size. Flake's looking at it, too. We both just look at it for a few minutes. I'm still thinking about changing clips. "Think we're really gonna do this?" I go.

Flake shrugs. He's still looking at the pistol. We hear some kids ride by on bikes, but we can't tell who they are. "Let's do this later," he says.

"Okay," I go.

We put everything back in their cases. At first the snaps on the outside of the big one won't close, but finally we get it. I push it into the closet while Flake puts the ammo away. When he gets back we fold up all the newspaper and look around to see if we missed anything.

"What do you want to do now?" Flake finally goes.

I'm as depressed as he is. "Who knows?" I go.

He takes the newspaper under his arm and leaves. I can hear him in the kitchen. When I get in there he's sitting at the table crying.

"We are such pussies," he goes.

I sit down across from him but there's nothing to say.

He sniffs and rubs his face and then cleans his hand and nose on a napkin from the napkin holder.

"Wanna play mosh volleyball?" I go.

"No," he goes.

"Wanna throw rocks?" I go. Sometimes we throw little rocks at cars from a sand-and-gravel lot where we can get a running start when we get chased.

"No," he goes.

"So what do you want to do?" I go.

He puts his head on the table and leaves it there for a few minutes. "All right, let's throw rocks," he goes.

On Monday at breakfast my mom tells me that the meeting with the vice principal and Ms. Meier is going to be tomorrow, which is the same day as Gus's birthday party.

"That should be festive," she says.

"The kid didn't do the scheduling," my dad goes. He's up early and looking at something on his laptop at the kitchen table.

"Can I try your coffee?" I ask him.

"Maybe you should try one bite of breakfast," my mom says.

"I ate one bite," I tell her.

"This graph is perfectly incoherent," my dad goes. He turns the computer to show me, then taps around on the keyboard.

"I hate when that happens," my mom says. She's rooting in a little bowl for change for my lunch money.

I move his mug closer and take a sip. It's so full I have to lean over it.

"Can I try?" Gus says.

"It's not good for you," my dad goes.

My mom reminds me I'm going to be late. She dumps the lunch money into an envelope and hands it over. I stuff it into my pack. "I hope you finished the rest of your homework," she says.

My dad looks at me when I come around from the other side of the table. "We gotta get you some new pants," he goes. "How often does he *wear* those pants?"

"Every day," my mom tells him.

"Oh, was I supposed to have noticed sooner than this?" he asks her.

"Don't you need a jacket?" she asks me.

"I'm all right," I tell her, but when I open the back door it's freezing.

"What about your homework?" she calls.

"I didn't need to do it all," I go.

"You going to say good-bye to your brother?" she asks.

"Bye, Edwin," Gus calls.

I poke my head back in. "How old you gonna be, Gus?" I ask him. "How old you gonna be on your birthday?"

He holds up the right number of fingers.

At the bus stop the ninth-graders leave me alone. Outside before the bell rings I don't see Flake. At the lockers I get mine open without much trouble.

In first-period English I get called on once and I know the answer. In second and third period I have a stomachache but it goes away. In math the teacher goes, "How many people didn't get to finish the whole worksheet?" and I raise my hand along with a few other kids and he just leaves it at that.

At lunch I make a joke in line about the chocolate pudding and Tawanda and another kid laugh. "Hey, how'd that World of Color project come out?" the other kid, a cross-eyed girl, wants to know. "Don't ask," Tawanda tells her. A kid who's holding everybody up looking for a cookie with chocolate chips instead of raisins has a booger hanging out of her nose and nobody tells her.

No Flake once I'm out of the line with my tray, so I sit by myself.

In fifth period two kids get into a fight before class as I'm coming through the door and I end up having to help break it up. They both get sent to the vice principal.

"Boys're like *dogs*," a girl by the window says, and everybody laughs.

"Well, girls're like . . ." a boy goes, and when he can't think of anything the class laughs again.

"I'm not going to be here Monday," another kid goes. Nobody's paying any attention. "I'm not going to be here Tuesday, either," he adds.

In sixth period a kid falls asleep and slides all the way to the floor before he wakes up. In seventh I watch the clock for twenty-two straight minutes until the bell rings. Flake isn't around before I get on the bus to go home, and nobody answers at his house when I call him from my room.

7

When they first brought Gus home from the hospital they had him in a little bassinet by their bed. When I couldn't sleep, instead of wandering around the house all night I'd creep in there and watch him move around. He looked like a little turnover. They left him right in the streetlight. I don't know how he went to sleep. He'd move for a while and get quiet and then move a little more. My mom slept with her face in the pillow and whimpered every so often. My dad always looked like he'd washed ashore in a storm. Sometimes I sat in the chair in the corner. Sometimes I went back to bed.

In the mornings we had this thing we did when we all woke up. When I heard Gus making his noises I got up and went into their room. By then he was in their bed between them, and I'd climb over my dad and get next to Gus. I'd push the mattress with my hand to make his head move. He kept an eye on me. He grabbed my hair when he could reach it.

I'd say, "Gus, do you *like* Mommy and Daddy?" and give the mattress a few pushes and it would look like he was shaking his head. My dad especially laughed. I think I was nine then.

"What's wrong, honey?" my mom would go sometimes. It always surprised me.

"Nothing's *wrong*," my dad would go. "Why does something have to be wrong?"

"Are you okay?" my mom would go. She'd be lying on her pillow looking at me over Gus's head. He'd reach for my hair and I'd tip toward my dad, to make him reach farther.

"I'm fine," I'd go.

"You seem worried," she'd go. Or "You seem sad." That happened five or six times.

"*Are* you worried?" she said one time a few hours later, when my dad was upstairs changing Gus.

"I guess," I said. It felt like I was always worried.

"About Gus?" she asked.

I must've looked so surprised that she asked if it was something else.

"You think you need to see somebody?" she asked another time. She meant like a psychiatrist. She was always frustrated that she never got anywhere with me.

"I had this dream where I rolled Gus down the stairs," I told them once at breakfast. "Except he did this stair-luge thing. Then we were all doing stair luge."

There was this pause before anything else happened. My dad had the paper, and my mom had her coffee mug halfway to her mouth.

"What's a stair-luge thing?" she finally said. She still had the mug up by her chin.

Like luge, like the Olympics, I told her.

Of course I couldn't explain so they both had a cow and a half though they tried not to show it. My mom spent the next week telling me how much everybody loved me and my dad dropped by my room every night before dinner to see how things were going. When they moved Gus into his own room that summer I'd go in there when I couldn't sleep. They had a big chair with a hassock next to his crib, and I liked to sit in it and stick a hand through the bars. My mom caught me in there once, in the middle of the night.

"You scared me," she said. Then she got all teary. She got a blanket and tucked me in. "I just wanted to *sit* in here," I remember telling her. I found out later that after I fell asleep she came back and took my picture.

Or maybe it's this: I remember we hiked up to this park on the top of a hill one Saturday in October when all the leaves were down. It was hot and we all had our sweatshirts piled on the back of Gus's stroller. We took turns pushing him up this steep path. It was so steep he was almost lying down. My dad joked about us getting nosebleeds. At the top there was this great view but a storm was coming so we couldn't stay long. Going back down I jumped on this tree branch to swing on it but slipped off and hit my head. I landed on the grass but it felt like cement. Everybody asked if I was okay and I thought I was. But later I kept feeling like I had to open my eyes wide and squeeze them shut. And when I shook my head it was like I was still shaking it when I stopped. I got more headaches after that, too. I was talking to Flake about it once when he complained that I got a lot of headaches and I told him about falling. I made it sound like I'd been higher up than I was. I told him I thought I might've really fucked up my head. I expected him to make a joke but instead he asked me all these questions like he was a specialist. He asked if I got dizzy for no reason. He asked if I saw all right. He asked if I got extra horny.

"What's that got to do with my head?" I asked him.

"You're fucked up normal," he said. "I don't think you're fucked up abnormal."

I knew what he meant, but since then I asked him if he

sleeps all right and he does. I think it depends on what day you catch me.

"You know what a clit is?" Weensie asks Flake out on the playground. We just got off the buses and it's raining a little, but everybody still wants to hang around outside.

Flake stands there strumming the seam of his pants with his thumb.

"I think he does," I go.

"You think he does?" Weensie goes.

"Duh," I go.

Dickhead wanders up. The two of them are wearing T-shirts with the same cartoon guy's face on them. Neither of us know what show it's from. Flake's eating a Go-Gurt, which is his breakfast.

"You know how many holes a girl's got?" Dickhead asks. I can't tell if he heard Weensie's question or not.

"Yeah," Flake goes.

"You do?" Dickhead says.

"Yeah," Flake goes. He squeezes the yogurt up into his mouth while he watches Dickhead.

"So how many?" Dickhead says.

"I know," Flake goes.

"So how many?" Weensie says. By this point three or four other kids have drifted over, thinking there may be a fight.

"Fuck off," Flake goes.

"He doesn't know," Weensie says.

"I think he does," Dickhead says. "I think he's got 'em himself."

I'm worried somebody's going to ask me.

Flake's maybe waiting for the bell, but if he is, it doesn't ring. "Three," he finally goes.

"Where are they?" Dickhead asks.

"He *said* three," I go.

"Where are they?" Dickhead asks.

"One in the front, and one in the back," Flake goes.

We're all standing there. He wraps the flattened Go-Gurt tube around his fingers.

"Where's the other one?" Dickhead goes.

"One on the side," Flake goes.

"The *side*?" Dickhead goes. "The *side*?" Weensie goes. "The *side*?" the other kids go. It starts raining harder. Flake goes for Dickhead's throat and knocks him onto his back on the pavement. Weensie takes a swing at my head, and when I grab his hair and pull him over me I can feel some of it tearing. He's screaming in my ear and the other kids stop saying "The *side*?" and start saying "Fight! Fight!" and Weensie and I try to kill each other until adults come along and break us up. "He pulled out some of my fucking *hair*," he screams at the vice principal, who's wrestling to keep him off of me. Flake and Dickhead are already gone, or I can't see them because of everybody else. Somebody's got me around the neck and it turns out to be the new gym teacher. He's got me so I can't breathe, and when I struggle he squeezes tighter.

"Well, this morning's episode will help focus our discussion," the vice principal says at the parent-teacher conference that afternoon. I've been suspended for a day and my mom's crying. My dad says her name and she stops. Gus's birthday party has been postponed. Gus is with a baby-sitter.

"His mother's upset," my dad tells the vice principal.

The vice principal moves the Kleenex box closer to her on the desk. He tells us that one of the teachers, Ms. Meier, wanted to be here as well and should be coming through the door momentarily. "As you can see, things aren't getting better," he says.

My dad nods like he can see that and would like to move things along a little faster. "Is he unusually problematic, or middle of the pack in terms of your experience with these kinds of problems?" he goes.

"Call me Justin," the vice principal goes.

"All right, Justin," my dad goes. "Is he unusually problematic, or kind of middle of the pack in terms of these kinds of problems?"

The vice principal gives him a smile. "I'm not sure I'm ready to handicap him like this is the Kentucky Derby," he goes.

"I thought I asked a straightforward question," my dad goes.

My mom asks if he could please stop it, and he apologizes. Maybe because he teaches in a college, you can see that he thinks that people who teach in junior highs are probably not all that smart.

"Can I ask what you've been noticing at home?" the vice principal asks. "In terms of behavior, in terms of the way he's been feeling?"

My mom talks for a while. My dad adds things in here and there. When they're finished they ask me if I think they left anything out.

"Sounds about right," I go.

Ms. Meier comes clumping down the hall and opens the door like she expected somebody was holding it shut. "Hello, hello, everyone," she goes. She asks to be called April.

"April Meier," my dad goes.

"That's it," she says.

"Nice to meet you," my mom goes. She sounds miserable.

"And you," Ms. Meier says. "What have I missed?"

The vice principal repeats what they told him about the

home situation. He leaves a few things out and screws one or two things up. "Is that about right?" he asks me.

"Yep," I go.

"Well. Here's what we've been noticing around *here*," Ms. Meier says. "May I start?" she asks the vice principal.

He makes a little *after you* gesture.

"Edwin acts like he's under constant pressure," she says.

"My little spray can," my dad goes, almost to himself.

"Is that a joke?" my mom goes.

"No," he tells her. She looks at him.

Ms. Meier waits for everybody to finish. "He's either very very quiet or acting out in various antisocial ways," she says. Everybody sits and looks at each other for a minute.

"Could you give us some examples?" my mom finally asks.

Ms. Meier gives them a few. Some I didn't even know she knew about. "He's got a good head on his shoulders," she says at the end. "He's very bright."

"He's bright, we know that," my dad goes.

"He's so bright," my mom goes.

"He's had trouble in math, but verbally he's tested off the charts," the vice principal says. "Is that your sense of him, as well?" he asks Ms. Meier.

"It is," she goes. "Though this year he seems to be actively working, in his essays, to rein in his vocabulary."

"Are you doing that?" my dad goes. "Are you working to rein in your vocabulary?"

Everybody looks at me. "I'm working to rein in everything," I go.

Nobody answers. They all look at each other. The vice principal smiles.

"How long have you been noticing this?" my mom goes. "This is a question for either of you, I guess. Do you have some idea when it started?"

"Don't pick at your fingernails," my dad goes to me.

The vice principal looks at Ms. Meier to see who's going to go first. "I've just started with Edwin," she says. "I didn't have him last year. But I've checked with Mrs. Fisher, and she said he tailed off badly in the spring."

"That's been my impression, too," the vice principal says. My dad jots a note to himself on a little pad of paper he's brought along. "Were there any traumatic events, or did anything in particular happen last spring that you guys know about?" the vice principal asks.

They think about it. They look at each other. "Not that I know of," my dad goes. My mom agrees with him.

"Was there anything in the spring you can remember that really affected you?" Ms. Meier asks me.

"No, not really," I go.

"But there *was* something?" my mom goes.

"No, not really," I go.

"You can't think of one thing?" my mom goes.

"Well, I got older," I go.

Everybody sits back in their chairs. The vice principal slides his palm back and forth on the desk blotter in front of him. He watches his hand while he does it.

"So where do we go from here?" my mom wants to know.

"Well, there are various options," the vice principal tells her. "One place to start is with a special-ed program we have for extra work with socialization. It meets one day a week during school hours and one day a week after school hours. So it's not too burdensome."

"You mean like for retards?" I go.

"I don't know what you mean," the vice principal says, mad.

"You mean like special-needs kids?" I go.

"Special-ed programs are just that," he goes. "They're for all sorts of things. Whatever someone needs extra help with."

"What's it involve?" my mom wants to know.

"It's mostly a workshop," the vice principal goes. "A workshop with his peers. Other kids who're also having difficulties. They're given tasks to perform together. They do skits and hypotheticals, stuff like that."

I imagine sitting across a table from Dickhead and Weensie and Hogan and every other asshole in the school and doing skits.

"Is that it? Is that all we're going to try, at first?" my dad goes.

"We also have worksheets and exercises to send home," the vice principal tells him.

Ms. Meier starts to say something, and my dad interrupts her. The vice principal lowers his head and holds up a palm to my dad and rotates his other hand to let her know it's her turn.

"We find the combination can work very well," she goes.

"Ms. Meier used to help out in the program," the vice principal tells us.

"That sound amenable to everyone?" he asks, after no one says anything for a while. "If you guys don't do the work on your end, it doesn't matter what we do here," he adds. "We can only do so much with the time *we* have him."

My dad lets out a huge amount of air. "Sounds fine with me," he says. "What about the patient?" he goes to me. "How's it sound to you?"

"Fine with me," I go.

"Fine with you," he goes. "Everything's fine with you."

"Well, I guess that's about it," the vice principal says. "Edwin, do you have anything that *you'd* like to add?"

"Nothing I can think of," I go. I stand up. My dad stands up.

"Mr. Hanratty," Ms. Meier says. "Does Edwin have a chemistry set?"

"Not that I know of," my dad says.

"Did we get him a chemistry set?" my mom asks.

"Not that I know of," my dad says.

My stomach feels like it jumped up and froze in midair. Ms. Meier moves her mouth back and forth like she's thinking.

"Why do you ask?" my dad goes. He sits back down.

"Edwin showed me something he was working on," she finally tells him. "Actually he didn't show me. It fell out of his backpack. He said it was from a chemistry set that you'd gotten him."

My dad turns to me. "What's the deal, Sport?" he asks.

"Are you a scientist at the college?" she asks.

"Economist," my dad goes. He looks back at me.

"What?" I go.

"What's she talking about?" he goes.

"I do these stupid drawings," I go. "They're just drawings."

"Did you tell her you have a chemistry set?" he goes.

"Yeah," I go.

"Why?" my mom goes.

"They're embarrassing," I go. Everybody's looking at me. I can't tell who believes me. "They're *embarrassing*," I go again.

"So you lied about it?" he goes.

"Yeah," I go.

My dad looks at Ms. Meier. "I don't know what to tell you," he goes. "You're not going to lie to her anymore," he says to me. "Right?"

"No," I go.

She looks at me for a minute and then turns to him and shrugs. "Well, we'll try and keep an eye on things," she tells him.

"So will we," my mom tells her. She stands up and Ms. Meier stands up and they shake hands. "Thanks so much," my mom goes. "And we're sorry for all the trouble."

"Oh, don't be sorry," Ms. Meier tells her. "We all want to do everything we can."

"What do you say?" my dad says to me. We're all up now and he's got a hand on my shoulder.

"Good-bye," I go.

The vice principal laughs.

"What else do you say?" my dad goes.

"Sorry," I go.

"It's all right, son," the vice principal says. He sticks out a hand and I give it a good shake. "Let's try and see a little less of each other for a while," he suggests.

"Definitely," I go. "And thanks again."

On the way home, my mom thanks me for thanking him. I tell them I'm sorry, and I am. She feels so much better that we have a kind of half-party with just us and Gus when we get home. Gus keeps going "So I get two parties?" while we dish out cake and some of the presents.

"That's right, hon," my mom goes. "You get two parties."

8

"It's all right to be queer, you know," Michelle tells Flake and me at lunch the next day. I'm not in the best of moods and neither is he.

"My sister in high school's in the Lesbian Alliance," she goes.

"What're you *talking* about?" Flake finally brings himself to say. Kids go back and forth past our table. It's another rainy day and everybody seems worn out by the suckiness of everything.

Lunch is spaghetti and meatballs and the spaghetti's cold. We've already eaten all the meatballs. I got a 40 on my math quiz. I had headaches all morning. A girl in English stared at me the whole period like I was a fingernail she found in her whipped cream.

"I *told* you," Tawanda says without looking up from her dish.

"What'd you tell her?" I go.

"*I* told her not to bring it up," Tawanda says.

Flake has his elbows on the sides of his tray and his fingers are pushing on his cheeks like they want to get in there.

Everyone calls us queer but they call us everything else, too. It wasn't like we thought anybody thought we *were* queer.

"My sister says we have the right to our own bodies," Michelle says.

Tawanda goes, "Girl, I don't think they're liking your helping hand, here."

"It was hard for my sister, too," Michelle explains to her. "She says she wishes somebody had talked to her."

Flake stares at her. She looks back. I feel like resting my head in the spaghetti. I settle for turning over the plate. Most of the sauce and noodles end up still on my tray.

Tawanda passes me a clump of napkins for the stuff that isn't. "*Some*body should've gotten the vegetarian casserole," she goes.

"You're sitting here and calling me queer?" Flake finally asks. The way he says it makes me even sadder. They're the closest things we had in the school to people who didn't hate us.

"It's not a judgment thing," Michelle tells him.

"If I called you a fuckin' skank, would you say that's not a judgment thing?" Flake goes.

Michelle doesn't answer.

"I hurt your feelings?" he goes.

She looks off toward the cafeteria line.

"I hurt her feelings," he goes to me. "She calls me a fucking queer, and *I* hurt *her* feelings."

"Where'd you get this shit?" I ask her. "Where'd you come up with this?"

"Forget it," Michelle says. "Forget I said anything."

"We're not going to forget it," Flake goes.

"Flake," I go.

"Fuck you too," he goes. "Hey," he goes to Michelle. He taps her arm. "Jizzbag."

"Get away from me," Michelle goes.

"Tell her she's gotta talk to me," he says to Tawanda.

"I ain't getting in the middle of this," Tawanda says. "I *fin-ished* my lunch."

"Tell her she's gotta talk to me," he goes again.

"Somebody said bad shit about you, we'd tell you who it was," I go to Tawanda.

She thinks about it and she knows I'm right. "Maybe we should tell them," she goes to Michelle.

Michelle's slurping from her milk pint. She's looking at it like it disappoints her. "I was just trying to help," she says. She's pissed off but looks embarrassed, too. When she's sitting she always takes her sandals off and turns them around with her toes and then puts her feet back on top of them.

"Who told you we were queer?" Flake goes. He's keeping his voice down but that's about it.

"Matthew Sfikas," Michelle finally says. "Him and another kid."

"Who the fuck is Matthew Sfikas?" Flake goes. You can hear him thinking; *I don't even* know *these people.*

"Oh, shit," I go. "He's that ninth-grader I had detention with."

"What's *his* fucking damage?" Flake goes. "Why's *he* doing this?"

"He said he saw you guys," Michelle goes. "That's the only reason I believed him."

"I told the monitor he was playing with himself," I go to Flake. "He's getting even."

"What did he say he saw us doing?" Flake goes. His voice is a little high. I'm getting as worried as the girls are.

"I don't want to talk about that," Michelle says.

Flake looks around like he's trying to find something to use on somebody. "Who is he?" he goes to me. "Point him out."

"He's not here right now," I go. I make like I'm looking and can see he's not here. He doesn't say a word from there on, and neither does Michelle.

"Nice dining with you all," Tawanda says when we get up from the table. Nobody answers.

"Isn't your class that way?" I go to Flake as we head down the hall.

He shoulders into a ninth-grader and the kid just gapes at him. "I'm not going to class," he goes. Then he turns a corner and the bell rings.

He gets detention for having spent fifth and sixth periods wandering around the school looking for Matthew Sfikas. He did his looking by peeking into ninth-grade classrooms one by one. Finally a teacher noticed and went out into the hall.

"You don't even know what he looks like," I tell him in the detention room. He's alone and there's one kid waiting outside the door for the monitor to show up. I only have a minute before the buses leave.

He sits there hanging on to the front end of his desk with both hands like the floor's gonna tip.

"Why get a hundred years of detention for *this* kid?" I tell him on the phone that night. "Why not just save him for our thing?"

"Save him for what?" he finally goes.

"Our thing," I go.

There's a little buzzing on the line. Nothing works right in either of our houses.

"He could be first," I go. "We could start with him."

"Yeah," Flake admits. I can tell he thinks it's a good point.

The next day before homeroom someone trips a seventh-grader when he's coming down the stairs with his art project. His art project is the Seattle Space Needle made out of elbow macaroni. Flake and I are at the bottom when he lands. Macaroni ricochets off lockers.

He sits there wailing and scooping up the pieces that are still glued together. He doesn't care who sees him. Kids with lockers nearby look sympathetic. Some kick macaroni back toward him.

"Somebody should help BG out, there," somebody from our grade goes. He got called Baby Gherkin after some kids saw him in the shower in gym.

A girl carries a bigger piece over and sets it down next to him. "Thank you," he goes.

People step around him going up and down the stairs, and he tries to fit a couple of the pieces back together.

When I see Flake before third period his middle finger is wrapped in this fat bandage. It looks like a Q-Tip. He's happy about it. He says they were doing dissection in science and he put the little plastic scalpel with the razor blade in his pocket. He only remembered when he put his hand in his pocket later. "Look what I did to my finger!" he says to the vice principal when he goes by while I'm standing there. Kids laugh. "Ouch," the vice principal goes. It looks like he's already heard about it. He doesn't seem to get that he's just been given the finger.

After lunch Flake spots me at the other end of the room and waves both hands. Both middle fingers are bandaged. When I ask him, it turns out that after he cut the first finger he stuck the scalpel in his other pocket.

"You gotta be fucking kidding me," I tell him.

"No," he goes, like he lucked out twice. "Hey, Mrs. Pruitt!" he calls. He sticks up both middle fingers.

After school we decide to walk home when Flake's detention is over. I sit on the steps and wait, watching the other kids with their friends. When he finally gets out we hang around the end of the playground for a minute before heading home. A ninth-grader comes up and asks if we want to buy any shit.

"What do you got in mind?" Flake goes.

The kid has a white kitchen garbage bag in his knapsack. He shows us the inside of it without taking it out. I can't tell if Flake knows what he's looking at.

"White crosses," the kid goes.

We look at them. You can tell Flake's thinking the kid might be fucking with us.

"What happened to your fingers?" the kid asks.

"What fingers?" Flake goes.

"Those," the kid says, pointing at the bandages.

"Boating accident," Flake goes.

The kid takes some time to work that out. "So you interested?" he finally says.

"How much?" Flake goes.

The kid tells him.

"I don't think so," Flake goes, like that's too much. The kid shrugs and twist-ties his bag and zips up his knapsack. He walks back over to his friends.

"You know what white crosses are?" I ask.

"You?" Flake goes.

"Yeah," I go.

On the way home Hermie comes running over from a side street. He must've seen us going by. "What happened to your fingers?" he asks Flake.

"Boating accident," Flake goes.

"Yeah, right," Hermie says. "That kid try and sell you something?"

"How do you know?" Flake goes.

"He's always ripping people off," Hermie goes.

"How'd you know he was trying to sell us something?" I go.

"I saw you," he goes.

A black Camaro goes by and does a U-turn and slows down when it reaches us. A girl hangs out the window and a much older guy is driving. "Eat shit, Herman," the girl goes.

"Fuck *you*," Hermie calls.

The guy guns the car and they peel out.

"My sister," Hermie goes.

"You got a sister?" Flake goes.

"I guess I must, if that's her," Hermie goes. I laugh.

"Shut up," Flake goes.

"Duh," Hermie says. Flake lets it go.

"So what happened to *you*?" I finally ask Hermie. He's got like a huge scuff mark on the side of his head. It's a black-and-red scab.

"Budzinski," Hermie moans. He touches the scab with his fingers like it's come off before.

"I'm gonna have to see this Budzinski," Flake says, like he's impressed.

We walk along for a while. Nobody says anything or asks where Hermie thinks he's going. You can see how happy he is about it.

"My dad's got a gun, you know," he goes.

"Everybody's dad's got a gun," Flake goes.

"I know where he keeps it," Hermie goes.

"I guess we're all in trouble now," Flake tells him.

I start to say something, but I don't even know what I was going to say. I'm such a loser and a half. I'm the kid you think about when you want to make yourself feel better. If I were me I'd talk about myself behind my back.

It rains for three straight days. One morning it's so dark that I think it's still nighttime until my mom comes upstairs and strips the covers off the bed with me still lying there. Flake's detention lasts until the end of the week, so when school's finally over I just go home and do homework.

The girl sitting next to me in homeroom cries all three days.

The teacher asked about it on the first day and they talked at the front of the room, but he hasn't brought it up since.

"Here he is, Mr. Greenpants," my math teacher says to everybody when I show up a minute late.

I spend the rest of the class not believing he did that to me.

Every Monday morning we have to hear on the PA system, along with the rest of the horseshit about blood drives and smoking on the playground, how JV football did. Half the kids cheer when it turns out we won. The principal always goes, "And in JV footbaaaaall . . ." and then waits, like it's a cliffhanger. It drives me nuts. It feels like it's six in the morning and these idiots are getting excited about a game they *saw* last Friday. Weeks when it turns out we lost, a few of us around the room cheer. "That's very nice," the homeroom teacher goes.

Our nickname is the Hilltoppers. The student newspaper has headlines like LADY TOPPERS O'ERTOP LADY PANTHERS. During Student Fair the first week of school when I found myself over by their table the editor asked if I'd be interested in working on the paper. He had no idea who I was. I told him I would if I got to do a Dirp column.

"Sure," he said. "What's a Dirp?"

"Dicks in Responsible Positions," I told him.

"Hey," he said to a kid standing right behind me. "You interested in working on the school paper?"

My dad had the same idea that week. He sat me down and gave me the college-and-extracurriculars talk.

"*College?*" I went. We were all in the kitchen and I was helping my mother break the ends off of green beans. "I'm still deciding if I'm going to *high* school."

"Very funny," he said.

When he sees me in the living room looking like death warmed over and staring out the window because school sucks and it's been raining for four years and Flake's been in detention all week, he goes, "Now, what do *you* want?" and makes a face at me. "*You* going to turn into an aggrieved minority group?"

"What?" I go.

"Your father had a bad day," my mom calls from the other room.

He disappears to change and seems like he's in a better mood when he comes back. He's carrying a beer and has his ready-to-talk look on.

"Given any more thought to the school paper?" he goes, like we were just talking about it. He's home from class or office hours or the Mascot Committee or whatever he had today, and he's got his beer and now he's ready to talk.

Gus wanders through the living room and hands him a carrot. "I don't want this," Gus says, and then leaves.

My dad takes a bite of the carrot and a swig of the beer. "I'm going to write a book about domestic life in America," he goes. "It's gonna be called 'Dads Eat What No One Else Wants.' "

"If you fell asleep on your back and it was raining hard enough, do you think you'd drown?" I ask him.

"No," he goes.

"I think you would drown," I tell him.

My dad eats his carrot. "You seem a little down," he goes.

My hands are holding up my chin. I let my head slip through them until they finally have to grab my hair.

"Your mother tells me the Nightrider's run afoul of the law," he goes.

"Yeah," I go.

"He's a misunderstood figure, there's no doubt about that," my dad goes.

I make a sound like a horse.

It makes my dad laugh. "Only in junior high can you be the object of awe *and* derision," he goes.

"What's *that* mean?" I ask.

He shrugs. He looks at his beer like he admires it. "Economics humor," he goes.

"Doesn't sound like economics," I tell him. I still haven't turned around from the window.

Gus is in the den singing to himself and playing with a toy that needs batteries and has no batteries. Lately he's been going around the house butchering one of his favorite songs from a kid's show he watches. The song's called "We All Sing with the Same Voice." He sings it "We all sing with the same boys."

"Remember that thing you hung on the Christmas tree?" my dad goes. He says it like he doesn't need an answer, and I don't say anything. It's raining even harder.

"It's like *blue* out," I finally go.

What he's talking about was last year when my English teacher told us at the beginning of a class that she'd just read the greatest short story in the history of the English language. She held up the book and hugged it to her chest. We were like, *Please*.

She read the beginning of it in this hushed voice.

"I'm so moved," this kid next to me whispered, and a few kids giggled.

There was one line that sounded right, though. I went up after class and asked if I could see it. It probably made her month.

The line was "Christmas came, childless, a festival of regret." I copied it down while she stood there. She asked if I wanted to read the whole story, and I told her I'd get it out of the library.

When we were decorating, I put the line on a star-shaped piece of paper and hung it on the tree. "What the hell is *this*?" my dad said when he finally found it.

9

Flake had the idea to bury something we wrote in a box for people to find like years later. There's a word for it but I forget what it is. He said it had to be a good box to keep the water out so what we wrote wouldn't rot. He said to work on what we were going to put into it. I'd work on mine and he'd work on his. Then we'd put our stuff in together. We don't know where we're going to bury it yet, now that we can't use our fort under the underpass. He thought it would be funny to put it next to the flagpole in front of the school, but I thought people would see where the ground had been dug up. He thought we could do it so nobody could tell.

I have a pad I've been writing stuff in and hiding in a space above where my top drawer fits into my desk. There's nothing on the cover but on the first page I wrote PROJECT with a pair of crossbones underneath. They look like an X. On the second page I have a score sheet divided into days of the times that people haven't looked at me or talked to me or answered me at school. I make a crossbones for each one and put them in a column. I fill it out when I get home from school or, if Flake comes home with me, before I go to bed. Mondays are ahead of Thursdays for first place.

On the third page I have a drawing of these huge Gatling guns they use in Chinook and Huey gunships. They fire like eight million rounds per minute. After that I have a drawing of Gus in sunglasses that I think is funny. I did it when he fell asleep in my room and I was supposed to be watching him. After that I have some demon faces that I can never get right.

After that there's a lot I still need to write down. Like: What happens when you hate yourself?

What happens when you know you're *worse* than anybody else knows you are?

What happens when everything you touch turns to shit?

What happens when you feel sorry for yourself and then sit around feeling sorry for yourself for feeling sorry for yourself?

Poor kids or kids who can't walk or pick up anything and have to work a computer with like sticks in their teeth: we're lucky compared to them. We're whiners. We're *babies*.

We're good at reminding each other how pissed off we are and how nobody cares, not really. Sometimes one of us'll whack the other on the side of the head to remind him of what we have to do.

So when we get his dad's guns and go into the assembly and we see like some special-ed kid in one of those chairs, do we bail and come back later when we hope there's only going to be people we hate around? We need to make sure that once we're in, we can't be going, Hey, watch out for Tawanda, or Let's not get Mrs. Pruitt, let's get Ms. Meier.

Flake says nobody's going to be taking him alive and that he's not going to shoot himself, either. I don't think we have to decide about that yet.

We might get away.

.   .   .

After a sign-up sheet for achievement tests went around the homerooms last week, he had us get out his father's guns again when the house was empty and he squatted on the bed and had us hold the Kalashnikov and the carbine up over our heads. Here's *my* achievement tests, he said. Here's yours.

GIRLS

Good stuff		*Bad stuff*
////	Monday	////////
/	Tuesday	////
//	Wednesday	/////
	Thursday	////
/	Friday	//

For the next fifty years, people who weren't anywhere around will swear they were right here when it happened. "So there I was, bullets flying." Shit like that. It makes us wish they *were* here. Then we could shoot them and they'd get what they want: proof they're not bullshitters.

Flake gives me a 50 percent chance of wussing out. He says if I do he'll shoot me himself. "I'll shoot *you*, you fuck," I tell him. It always makes him laugh.

He says to remember that out of everybody in the gym there's still only going to be two kinds of people: the ones who don't know anything about us, and the ones who don't want to know.

10

He hasn't given up on Matthew Sfikas. I can see his brain going, trying to figure something out. When I tell him again about my idea about waiting he goes, "I'll kick his ass now, *and* we can shoot him later."

"How are you going to kick anybody's ass with two fingers like that?" I want to know.

"I'll use a shovel," he goes. "I'll use a rake."

"You can't use a *shovel*," I go. "You can't use a rake."

"What do you care?" he goes. "I'll use a chain saw if I want." He won't, though.

"So let's find him then," I go. "Bring your rake."

"You think I won't?" he asks.

But then we end up just sitting in his room, and he's in a bad mood for the rest of the day.

"Why don't you put bug powder in his milk?" I go. I'm looking at the booklet that comes with his *Great Speeches* CD. Something knocks me to the floor on my face, and he's jumping up and down on my back with his knees.

I scream for him to quit it when I can, but he doesn't and finally I'm able to twist around and get him on the side of the head with my fist. Once he's off I keep using my right hand and he blocks it with his arm but not completely because he's trying to protect his finger. He straight-arms me in the mouth with the heel of his palm. Then we both go nuts.

His mom runs upstairs and separates us. It takes her some time, and she ends up with a scratched face. We're screaming at each other and she's screaming at us. One of his fingers is bleeding through the bandage.

"Fucking *maggot*," he keeps screaming.

"Suck *me*," I scream back.

"*Stop* it, *both* of you," his mom screams. We still won't stop trying to beat on each other, so finally she drags me downstairs by the collar. "Don't come *back* here, you fuck," he yells down the stairs. "*Fuck you*," I yell back up. "*Stop* it," his mom yells, shaking me so hard that she almost breaks my neck. She shoves me out onto the driveway and slams the back door.

She calls my parents while I'm walking home.

"I hear you and the Nightrider thought you were in the Thunderdome," my dad says when I walk in the door.

"I don't know what that means," I go.

"Are you all right?" my mom wants to know. I look in the mirror in the bathroom. My teeth are bloody and there's dried blood on my chin and some on my shirt. My back hurts where he was jumping on it. My lip's cut up again. Otherwise I'm fine. I feel like I'm going to cry, but that's out of frustration.

"It's all right," my mom says when she sees my face once I finally come back out of the bathroom. I stand there in the middle of the kitchen like I got a load in my pants. My dad knows enough not to say anything.

"Want me to help you with your face?" she goes.

"Yeah," I go. And start crying.

"It's okay," she goes. She comes over and puts her arms around me.

"Fucking asshole," I go, barely able to understand myself. I hang on to her for a minute.

"Hey," my dad says, about the language. My mom tells him to shush. Gus is up in their bedroom watching videos and misses the whole thing.

I don't call Flake or hear from him for a week. He wanders by in the hall a few times at school. I get up in the morning, get my stuff together and head for the bus. I come home, go up to my room and dump my stuff on the floor. I do homework. I do better than the teacher expected on a social studies quiz.

My dad asks a few days into this if I want to play catch. The next night my mom calls up the stairs that there's a special on about naval firepower.

After I'm supposed to be asleep I walk around the house without turning on the lights. I take the Bible out of their down-stairs bookcase and read it in the afternoons. I think about copy-ing down parts but never get around to it. I like Leviticus and Revelations. I look at the pictures in *African Predators*. There's one of a leopard that got ahold of a baboon. The baboon's face is being squeezed shut by the bite.

"So now you're not eating?" my dad asks after a while.

Gus comes into my room and sits with me sometimes, then goes out again.

"Can I tell you something?" my dad says, another time, at dinner.

"No," I go.

Finally, after a week and a half, I call Flake's house. The phone rings and rings and no one picks up.

In the mornings when I look in the mirror to comb my hair it looks like I have two black eyes.

My dad sits there while I have breakfast. He asks how I'm sleeping. I tell him I have no idea.

Hermie starts hanging out with me before the homeroom bell rings in the morning. He doesn't say anything about Flake. At first he doesn't say much at all.

"Listen, you gotta help me get back at Budzinski," he finally goes.

"Who *is* this kid?" I go.

He points across the playground but there's like forty kids where he's pointing.

It's about the third day he's been hanging around, and we're both watching other kids have fun. A bunch of them are seeing how many it takes to clog the tunnel slide for the grammar school. They're falling out and getting stuck and everybody's screaming.

He scratches his back through his SCREW THE SYSTEM shirt.

"You ever wash that?" I ask him.

"My mom does," he goes. "You ever wash those?" he says about my pants.

Near the window where Flake and I broke in I can see the girl who was crying three straight days last week. She's creeping around trying to sneak up on a pigeon. The pigeon keeps walking just out of her reach.

"You don't look so good," he goes. I make a face and he drops the subject.

Two other girls are standing there making fun of the one who's creeping around after the pigeon. Every so often she looks over when she doesn't think they're looking. She's the kind of girl who follows along with all the conversations and smiles whenever she gets noticed. The sun comes out and the whole playground gets warmer.

"So would you help me?" he goes.

"Help you what?" I go.

"With Budzinski," he goes.

"I'm not gonna help you beat up some sixth-grader," I tell him.

"I don't want you to help beat him up," he goes. "I just need help with a plan."

"A plan," I go. "Just hide behind a bush and hit him with a stick."

"That's a plan?" Hermie goes.

"He's a *sixth-grader,*" I go. "Take his candy. Push him down in the sandbox."

This pisses him off so much he shuts up for a while.

"I went *after* him with a stick," he finally goes.

"You went after him with a *stick*?" I ask him.

"He took it away and hit me with it." He looks ashamed.

This is what my life has come down to. I'm talking to sixth-graders about who beat who with a stick.

Hermie's tearing up, just thinking about it.

"Hey, it happens," I tell him.

"No it doesn't," he goes. "Not to anyone else."

"I get my ass kicked all the time," I tell him. "Are you kidding?"

He wipes his face and looks at his feet. He has an expression like getting compared to me isn't a help.

The bell rings for homeroom.

"*Some*body's gotta do something," he goes as we stand up and head inside. We get shoved aside by everybody who's more anxious than we are to get in.

"I'm gonna get the gun," he tells me the next day before homeroom. "Let's see what he does then."

"What are you talking about?" I ask.

"Let's see what he does then," he goes.

"What, you're gonna get your dad's gun and *shoot* him?" I go. I have this whirling in my stomach. I even put my hand on it.

"They'll know they can't fuck with me," he goes.

"Of *course* they can fuck with you," I go. "You're like two feet tall."

He looks out over the playground like it'd be hard to stop with just Budzinski.

"Don't talk stupid," I tell him. I don't know what else to say.

"I'm not talking stupid," he goes.

"It sure sounds like it," I tell him.

"No it doesn't," he goes.

Two fat girls are two steps down from us on the front stairs. "Which is better, an A or an A minus?" one goes.

"What're you *talking* about?" the other one goes.

"I got this," Hermie tells me. He shows me a knife inside his backpack. It's one of those knives you use to clean fish.

"What are you doing?" I go. "Are you fucking nuts?" He puts the knife down at the bottom of his pack and pulls out one of his school folders. "Are you fucking nuts?" I ask him again. "Bringing that to school?"

He starts pulling papers out of the folder, looking for something, spreading everything out so he can see. Some slide down the steps.

I stop one that's about to blow away. "You can't just get a gun," I tell him.

He keeps looking for whatever it is. He's not making much progress.

"You hear me?" I ask him.

"Leave me alone," he goes. He's crying again. Then he slips and the whole folder dumps open. Assignments and worksheets slide down the cement. They're filled with *X*s and red marks. The homeroom bell rings. He's scrambling around trying to get everything before the stampede reaches the stairs. I help with some papers right around me. A kid who's running past doesn't see him bending down and decks him. They both go flying. It's a big hit with the kids who have a view of it.

I help him up and he shakes loose and gets the rest of his papers and carries them into the building in a mess under his arm.

He doesn't show up the next day once I'm off the bus and hanging around. That night it occurs to me while I'm patrolling the house that we could be in real trouble if this nimrod takes out a gun and waves it around at school. That could be the end of our plan. Though I don't even know if our plan is still on. This occurs to me while I'm sitting in the living room in the dark watching cars drive by down the street.

I get like one hour's sleep. The next morning I circle the playground, but Hermie's not there and neither is Flake.

In English we all have to sign a poster that covers a whole cabinet wall and says "English 8: In Our Own Words." The last four sentences at the bottom are

I want to succeed in high school, but I know it will be a challenge.
I am not a loser. (Somebody's already crossed out the not.)
I will be a nobody to most and a somebody to a few.
In 8th grade, I am a nervous student.

I find a clear spot and sign "*F.U. Verymuch*" so only I can read it. Bethany, the girl Flake was talking about, comes up to me after class in the hall and hands me a folded piece of pink paper. When she lifts her hand her wristwatch always slides down practically to her elbow. She's carrying a zebra-skin pencil case.

"What's this?" I go.

"It's for you," she says, and her friends watch and giggle. I read it on the way to math.

PSYCHOLOGY TEST

I like

A) big gloppy desserts and frosting	B) fruit
A) hot sex	B) good talks
A) $$$$$$$$$	B) good friends
A) boys	B) girls

I'm pissed that I was excited there for a minute because a girl was giving me a note. I almost ball the thing up and throw it away, but I don't.

Bethany and her friends follow me while I'm reading. It makes me paranoid. I spend two periods thinking about what to do with it. Finally, since I'm alone again at lunch, I fill it out. I write "with" after "hot sex" and draw an arrow to "fruit." I write "with" after "good talks" and draw an arrow to "big gloppy desserts." I draw an arrow from "girls" to "$$$$$$$," and just leave "boys" and "good friends" blank.

I give it back to her when I go to bus my tray. In line I can see her and her friends leaning over it like it's a treasure map.

"You are so weird," she says to me later in the hall.

In seventh period the teacher's late and all the guys sitting around me are talking about hard-ons.

After school when I get home I call Flake again. This time he answers the phone.

"We got a problem," I tell him after he says hello. He hangs up.

I look at the phone and beat on the cradle part of it with the receiver.

"What's going *on* down there?" my mom wants to know. She's up in Gus's room getting him up from his nap.

I wait another day before calling again. "Don't hang up,

fuckhead," I say when he says hello. I don't hear anything after that. "Hello?" I go.

"I'm still here," he says.

"We got a problem," I tell him.

"So I hear," he goes.

"You already know?" I ask.

"You just told me," he goes.

I'm quiet, thinking about hanging up myself.

"So what's the problem?" he asks.

I imagine pulling the phone off the wall and beating it flat with the mallet my dad keeps in the basement. Living by myself for the rest of my life, and having no friends. "Our pal Hermie says he's getting a gun to go after that kid he hates," I go.

Flake laughs.

"I don't think he's just bullshitting," I tell him. It sounds like I just wanted an excuse to call, which pisses me off more than it should. "He had a knife in his pack on Thursday," I add.

"What kind of knife?" Flake wants to know.

"A big one," I go. "The kind you use on fish."

"On *fish*?" he says.

"His dad does have a gun," I tell him. "And Dipstick knows where it is. *And* he's a crazy fuck."

"Well, that's true," Flake admits.

"I'm thinking he'd screw it up for us," I tell him.

Flake's quiet, thinking about it.

"Hello?" I go.

"Maybe he would," he goes. "That's certainly the kind of shit that always happens to us," he adds after a minute.

"So?" I go.

"So what'd you tell him?" he asks.

"I told him not to talk stupid," I go.

He sneezes. "What else you tell him?" he asks. I hear him wiping his nose.

"I told him he couldn't just get a gun," I go.

My mom comes into my room and sits down. No knock, nothing. I wave her out. She shakes her head. "We have to talk," she whispers, exaggerating her mouth movements, I guess so I can read her lips.

"What'd he say?" Flake wants to know.

"He didn't say anything," I tell him.

"Hmm," he goes.

"Who're you talking to?" my mom mouths.

"I think we gotta talk to him," I go.

"I'll talk with him, all right," Flake goes.

"I gotta go," I tell him.

"Think he'd really do it?" he asks.

"I gotta go," I tell him again.

"What's the matter?" he goes.

"Is that Flake?" my mom asks in a regular voice.

"Is that your mother?" Flake goes.

"Yeah," I go, to both of them.

"She been listening this whole time?" he asks.

"No," I tell him.

"Jesus Christ," he goes, like there's no end to my stupidity. "Call me back, asshole." He hangs up.

It turns out my mom wants to talk about my dad. She's worried about him because he's worried about me.

I listen to her outline the problem for a while. The whole thing depresses me.

"You have anything to contribute?" she finally asks.

I shrug, which is not what she was looking for. She gives me a look and tells me more stuff about how sad he's been. He hasn't been sleeping either, or working on his book.

"I'm sorry about that," I tell her. Because I am.

"I realize it feels like you have a lot to deal with right now," she goes.

Feels like? I think: *I shouldn't get mad.*

She says she has a proposal. The family should go some-where for Thanksgiving, somewhere cool. Have Thanksgiving somewhere else, for once.

"Does that sound like a good idea?" she wants to know. She pulls her hair back behind her head and holds it tight with both hands. She doesn't let go.

"It sounds good," I tell her. She asks where we should go.

I don't have a lot of ideas right there and then.

"Where would *you* like to go?" she asks. "Wherever it is, it'd be nice to surprise your dad." She has this look on her face like she's carrying something that already spilled.

"The beach," I tell her. "Somewhere warm." I have no idea where that came from.

"The beach," she says, surprised. I can see her already thinking about it. "All right, the beach."

I'm still amazed by what comes out of my mouth some-times, but it doesn't matter. By Thanksgiving, everything'll have changed.

"We had a good talk," I hear her tell my dad. They're down-stairs with the TV on, and she keeps her voice low.

"Remember the summer we went to Six Flags?" Flake says, instead of hello, when he calls back. "My parents took us?"

"Yep," I go. It's eleven o'clock on a school night, and I'm dripping. I was taking a shower because I was bored. I can't decide whether to wash the rest of the soap off or consider the shower over.

Toward the end of the day we got stuck on the Ferris wheel about twenty feet off the ground. It just stopped turning. Some guys came to work on it below us. We were up there so long the sun started to go down. We could see some girls from our grade, including Bethany, in the car across from us. Flake had had a shitload to drink and had to piss superbad. He waited as long as he could and then grabbed a big cup on the floor of the car and let go. The cup filled up and he was still pissing. "Take it, take it," he said to me. "No fucking way," I said back and finally he had to stand up, still pissing, and throw the cup. It got all over both of us. The people in the car below us screamed. The guys working on the Ferris wheel yelled up at us that they were going to kill us once they got us down. The girls told everybody they ever knew once we got back, and then those people told everybody *they* ever knew.

"Why you bringing that up now?" I go.

My dad comes up the stairs and looks at me in the hall. He turns around and goes back down. "Your son's standing around balls naked dripping on the carpet," I hear him tell my mom.

"What were we, in fifth grade?" Flake asks. "I always think about that day."

"Why?" I go. I can think of lots of days that were equally bad.

"I don't know," he goes. "I don't know what it is about it."

My mom comes to the bottom of the stairs and looks at me for a while. "Your brother's *sleeping*," she tells me.

I don't know why I'm still in the hall. I go into my bedroom and shut the door.

She comes upstairs and opens the door a crack. "Get something on," she says. "You're gonna catch pneumonia."

"Is it because Bethany was there?" I ask Flake.

"Nah," he goes. It sounds like it hadn't occurred to him.

"Get something *on*," my mom goes.

"Hey, did Bethany give you something today?" I ask. "Like a note?"

"No," he goes.

"Yesterday?" I go.

"No," he goes.

He doesn't ask what I'm talking about.

My mom opens the door wider and comes in and drags a sweatshirt out of my dresser and pulls it over my head. I have to switch hands with the phone when she stuffs my arms in the sleeves. Then she goes downstairs and leaves me there, in a sweatshirt and no underpants.

The next morning Flake finds me before I'm even completely off the bus. "Let's go talk with Tiny Tot," he says.

The sixth-graders hanging around the baseball backstop see us coming and keep an eye on us. Hermie's not around and we don't feel like asking anybody where he is. Flake heads off to the front of the building and sure enough, we find him there in a tree.

"What's up, Screw the System?" Flake calls up to him.

"Nothing," Hermie says. He's trying for nonchalant but he's happy and worried that we came looking for him.

This was a bad move, I realize, standing there. Now whenever he wants our attention he'll go back to the gun thing. I put my hands in my pockets and there's a hole I never noticed. Two fingers go through to my leg.

Most of the leaves are still on the tree so when he moves his expression's hard to see. He's trying to climb but you can hear his sneakers slipping on the bark. Little twigs and dead leaves float down like snowflakes.

"Are those *lights* on your sneakers?" Flake goes.

Hermie doesn't answer him.

"Hear you're still having trouble with that kid," Flake goes.

"What kid?" Hermie says.

"You want our help or not?" Flake asks him.

"What're you going to do?" Hermie asks him back.

I look at Flake. I'm a little curious myself.

"We'll deal with it," Flake goes.

There's a big slipping sound and Hermie falls a few feet. A couple heavy branches swing a little. "Ow," he goes. I can see him rubbing something. "Why're you guys helping *me*?" he asks.

"That's what we do," Flake goes. He holds up both his bandaged fingers to the school. "We help people."

Hermie laughs.

"I say something funny?" Flake goes.

"Yeah," Hermie says.

"So point him out to us," Flake goes.

"What're you going to do, poke him in the eye with your bandage?" I ask. He gives me a look.

"I hurt my butt," Hermie complains.

"That's the bell," Flake goes, though I didn't hear it. "Show us who this kid is after school."

"I think I broke my butt," Hermie says.

Flake jogs to the front doors and I follow him. "I know how that feels," I call back to Hermie.

"Hey, help me get down," Hermie shouts, right before the doors shut behind us.

Flake and I get a chance to talk between second and third periods.

"We gotta only talk about the kid," Flake goes. "If we talk about the gun, it'll make it a big deal."

"That's what I was thinking," I tell him. He nods. "But we can't go beating up sixth-graders," I tell him. He nods again, like he thought of that, too.

He's kind of a hero for the rest of the day because word gets out that when they took the class picture for the eighth grade, homeroom by homeroom on the bleachers in the gym, at the last minute he held up both his bandaged fingers. Everybody's figuring it'll come out in the photos. Everybody's coming up to him in the halls and congratulating him, even ninth-graders and assholes like Dickhead and Weensie. After school he's in a really good mood.

"Hear you gave them the finger in the photos," Hermie says when he finds us outside. The buses are starting to fill up.

"Yeah, whatever," Flake goes. "So where *is* this kid?"

"Over here," Hermie says, and leads us two buses over. He points to a kid sitting in the back window. He doesn't try to hide that he's pointing him out to us.

"*Him?*" Flake goes. The kid looks smaller than Hermie, if that's possible. "I can barely see his head in the window."

"I didn't say he was a giant," Hermie says, insulted. "I said he beats me up."

Flake looks at me like somebody's asking us to gang up on Gus. "We're on the job," he goes to Hermie. "Mr. Hermie's sleeping well from tomorrow night on."

"Herman," Hermie tells him.

"Herman," Flake tells him back.

"So listen," Flake says to Budzinski once we get him alone. After we found his house we watched him shoot baskets with some of his tiny friends. They hacked around for an hour and a half and I think they made three baskets. They saw us watching. When the other kids finally left we walked over. Budzinski took one more sad hook shot and then put the basketball away and came out of the garage with a hammer.

"Feel like driving some nails?" Flake goes.

"What do you want?" Budzinski says.

"Can I see that?" I ask him, like I've never seen a hammer before. Budzinki hands it over.

So the three of us are standing in his driveway with me holding his hammer. Somebody looks out the window screen near the back door.

I hold up the hammer like that's the reason we came over. "This is a beaut," I tell him.

"So listen," Flake goes.

"I'm listening," Budzinski tells him.

They look at each other.

Flake makes this grin like he wants to pound the kid's head in. "You know that kid Herman?" he asks.

Budzinski just looks at him.

"About your size?" Flake asks.

"Yeah," Budzinski finally goes.

"He's a friend of ours," Flake tells him.

"Yeah?" Budzinski says. He sounds interested.

"Well, we watch out for him sometimes," Flake goes. "He's such a doofy little shit."

"You got that right," Budzinski says. He looks like he's trying to decide whether or not to laugh at us. If he does Flake'll take the hammer out of my hand and kill him right in his own driveway.

"He can be a pain in the ass sometimes," Flake goes.

"You got that right, too," Budzinski tells him.

"We were hoping you'd cut him some slack for the next few weeks," Flake says.

"Why should I?" Budzinski goes.

"Because if you don't we'll kick your ass," Flake tells him.

"I'll kick *your* ass," Budzinski tells him back.

The top of the kid's head comes up to like Flake's armpit. "Is the whole sixth grade fucking nuts?" Flake asks me.

"Get out of my yard," Budzinski goes. *"Mom!"* he calls.

"What's the matter?" his mother says from behind the screen in the window.

"Get outta my yard," Budzinski goes again.

"We tried to ask you nice," Flake tells him.

"I'm calling the police," Budzinski's mother says through the screen.

"Call the police," Flake tells her. "Call the fucking National Guard."

"Don't you talk to me like that," his mother says. She leaves the window and shows up at the back door. "What's your name?"

"Ed Gein," Flake tells her. "Tell the police Ed Gein was here and that he wants your son."

"And what's your name?" she says to me.

"Richard Speck," I tell her.

"Gimme my hammer back," Budzinski tells me.

I throw it into the yard.

"Asshole," he goes.

"I'm dialing," his mother says from inside the house.

The garbage cans at the end of the driveway are empty but Flake kicks them over anyway.

"That didn't work out too well," I tell him on the way home.

"Now he's *really* gonna go after Hermie," Flake says to himself.

I just keep walking. The hole in my pocket is bigger.

"Fucking cocksucking motherfucking dickbag dildo cunt-suckers," Flake goes.

I don't have much to say to that so I let it go. He makes the same point a few more times on the way home.

"We gotta move our thing up," he finally says, right before I head off for my house.

"I know," I go.

"We gotta pick a time," he tells me.

"I know," I go. My insides are screwed up thinking about it.

"Come over tomorrow night," he goes.

"Yeah," I go. And it feels like summer vacation was over just because somebody said so.

11

No sleep.

In the middle of the night I remember a math test I forgot about. There's still plenty of time to study before people get up. I know some of what I need to but just stare at the pages. I clear off the kitchen table and sit with just the hall light on. The house is quiet. My math book smells. The numbers and unknowns in chapter 3 jump from place to place after a while. On one problem I keep seeing a 5 where there's an X. $120/3 = 40$ miles $- 10/1$ hr $= 30$ miles/ 1 hr $450/30 = 15$ hrs. I shut my eyes for stretches. The refrigerator makes its little noise. Solve for X.

I read Isaiah in the Bible but don't like it as much.

I nod out once it's getting light and wake up in time to go upstairs before my mom gets up. I keep yawning and stretching my mouth to get some feeling back into it. "You're dressed already," she says when she opens my door to wake me.

I remember part of a football game I played in with some kids like a year ago.

"Eat something. Even if it's candy," my dad goes once he

sits down at the table. I'm still staring at my eggs. It's a weird feeling, like the right words or numbers are standing around just out of reach. My eggs look weird, too.

The meeting with Flake's tonight. I'm thinking, *if I could just close my eyes from now till then.*

"Hey. The *bus*," my mom tells me. She's leaning forward and has her hands on her thighs. Apparently she's said this already.

On the bus for some reason I think about summer camp when I was little. We put on a play. *12 Angry Men*.

"Seen Hermie?" Flake asks before homeroom. The ninth-graders are playing some kind of You're It game with a willow switch. It looks like it hurts.

I shake my head.

"Can you talk?" he goes. I nod a couple times. "I gotta go to the dentist after school," he says. "So just come over after supper."

I nod again. My cheeks are numb.

"My mom thinks I gotta get braces," he goes. He's smiling because he's thinking, Well, *that's* not gonna work out.

The Kalashnikov's heavy. I don't know if it's got a really big kick or if I can even hold it steady or what. Well, you'll find out, I say to myself when the homeroom bell rings.

There's an announcement about an assembly sometime this week. I miss when.

"When'd they say it was?" I ask the girl next to me.

She looks at me.

"When'd they say it *was*?" I ask her again.

"Mr. Hanratty, *what* is the problem?" my homeroom teacher goes. Everybody's got their mouth open, with this look. I'm surrounded by fish.

She sends me to the vice principal. We should've tested the guns before we did this, I tell myself while I'm walking down the hall. Now we're not going to have time.

I space out during my math test. Halfway through, the teacher stops in front of me and goes, "Mr. Hanratty, do you have something to write with?" "No," I go, and he gets me a pencil.

"I got a question for you," Tawanda says when we pass in the hall.

After fifth period I can't get my locker open again.

Before seventh I go to the nurse and tell her about the headache. Almost nobody goes to the nurse seventh period because you're almost home.

"What's it feel like?" she asks, interested.

I make claws and put both of them up around my eyebrows.

She has me lie down on a little cot with a facecloth over my head.

While I'm lying there I hear the vice principal. He keeps his voice down but I can still hear him. "Our friend with the nose is having a tough day, isn't he?" he goes.

"Headache," the nurse tells him. She shakes me a few minutes before the end of the period so I can get to my locker and still make the bus.

"We don't even know what we're going to do about the doors," Flake says as soon as I come into his room that night.

"I know," I go.

He's lying on his back in his underwear with his arm over his eyes. One of his bandages is soaked with dried blood.

"You bang your finger again?" I go.

He doesn't answer. "I got the guns out by myself," he finally says. "I think I know about the safeties and everything now."

"Good," I go. It's nice to have some good news.

"Sit down," he tells me.

There's an open jar of peanut butter on the chair. I pick it up and ask where the top is.

"What is it with you and stupid questions tonight?" he goes.

I roll the jar under his bed. It keeps going until it hits the wall. "This place is a shithole," I tell him.

"You mean this town?" he asks. He sounds worn out.

"You gonna keep your arm over your face all night?" I go.

"What do you care?" he goes. "You showing off your outfit?"

It's quiet. I move my feet back and forth while he lies there like he's dead. "You gonna play one of your speeches?" I ask.

"No," he goes.

His mom's screwing around with the blender downstairs. She was setting it up when I came through the kitchen. Now it sounds like she's trying to grind rocks.

"How was the dentist?" I go.

He grins without moving his arm off his eyes. "I need braces," he goes.

"When're you supposed to get 'em?" I go.

"Turns out I got an overbite," he goes. He finally takes his arm off his face and sits up. His neck is against the headboard.

"Is that comfortable?" I go.

He looks away and shakes his head. "So did you see our friend today?" he asks. "Or that other fucking midget? Budzinski?"

"Nope," I go. "But that doesn't mean they weren't there."

He makes a face.

"So what're we gonna do?" I go.

"First thing we gotta do is solve the door problem," he tells me.

"When's the assembly?" I go.

"Friday, fourth period," he goes. "You finish the stuff we're gonna bury?"

"Pretty much," I go. "You?"

He gets up and roots around in his closet. There's a little poop stain showing through his underwear. He throws shirts and shoes out into the middle of the room, then comes out with a pile of papers like a phone book.

"You're gonna bury all that?" I ask him.

He looks proud.

"What is it?" I go.

"None of your fucking business," he goes. The first page is all filled with writing. He holds the pile in front of me before he puts it back in the closet. He's careful about how he hides it again. Then he throws the shirts and shoes back in over everything he's arranged.

I had like five pages to bury, so now there's that to feel bad about.

"A *wedge*," he goes. "Jesus Christ. A wedge." He's still standing next to the closet.

I don't get what he's talking about.

He bunches his fingers together and makes a little move with his hand to demonstrate. "To seal up the side door. We do it from the *outside*. From outside the gym, in the hall. One of us brings a little wedge and a hammer. *Bang*, you drive it in under the door. Nobody from the *in*side can open it."

I'm still looking at him, trying to figure it out.

"We wait till everybody's in the gym. Then one of us does that," he goes.

"Where do we get a wedge?" I go.

"A *wedge*," he goes. "Anywhere. You *make* one. It takes two seconds."

I think about it. It makes sense. "So we gonna test it?" I go.

"We don't have to *test* it," he goes. "It's a *wedge*. What're we, testing to see if a *wedge* works?" He flops down onto the bed again, happy. "I can't believe I didn't think of it before. I can't believe even *you* didn't think of it."

I have a new headache or else the same one that just keeps coming back. "So this means we can do it Friday?" I go. But he's already thinking about something else. He's excited again. "You gonna have trouble with your fingers?" I go. Meaning with the guns.

He shakes his head, still thinking about whatever the other thing is.

"Roddy? Homework?" his mom calls up the stairs. We both jump.

"He's just going," Flake calls.

We listen for her leaving the bottom of the stairs.

"Do we know how much kick these guns have?" I go.

"Listen to you: Joe Pro," he says. "How much kick."

"Well, who knows," I tell him. The headache makes me squint.

"Just hold on to it," he tells me back. "Don't hold it like a faggot and you'll be fine."

"I'm not gonna hold it like a faggot," I tell him.

"Then we'll be fine," he goes. "Look, you better go."

I get out of the chair. "What about the thing with Hermie?" I go.

He does a thing with his hand like bugs are around his head. "We gotta stall him for a week," he goes. "Lemme think about it."

"You think about it, too," he tells me, after I say I'll see him later.

I don't come up with anything that night. Instead I spend a lot of time thinking about Bethany. I make up this little scene where she comes over and I go, "Hi. What are you doing here?" and she doesn't say anything but she pulls me into my garage and then puts her hand on my face.

I whisper to myself. A hard-on that's so hard it hurts comes and goes. We haven't figured out what we're going to carry the guns in, either.

When I get off the bus at school I'm so tired I have trouble focusing.

"What's the matter with *you*?" Flake goes.

"Your mother kept me up," I go.

"Your mother kept my dog up," Flake goes. He puts his arm around me like we're the best of pals and walks me over to the steps where we broke in.

"What's the longest anybody ever had a headache?" I go.

"So listen," he goes. "I think I solved the Hermie problem."

"What'd you do?" I ask.

"Stop yawning," he goes.

"I can't help it," I go.

"What if we tell him we'll get him something supercool that he can fight Budzinski with?" he goes.

"Like what?" I go.

"I don't know. Something supercool," he goes.

"Like what?" I go.

"How should *I* know," he goes. "Like nimchucks."

"Nimchucks," I go, thinking about it.

"We don't have to actually *get* any," he goes. "We just *say* we will."

"Why can't Budzinski take his nimchucks away from him and beat on him like he did with the stick?" I go.

"Ah, shit," Flake goes.

"That's what Hermie'll say," I tell him.

"Well, *you* come up with something, then," he says.

"I'm just saying what Hermie'll say," I tell him.

The homeroom bell rings. "So come up with something," Flake says again. We walk over and shove into the group that's heading in. "I'm doing all the work here."

When I see Hermie in the hall between first and second period he's got a black eye.

"Shit," Flake says when I see him before third period. "You talk to him?"

"I just saw him," I tell him.

"We gotta find him at lunch," Flake says. "And we gotta talk to him after school."

I get my math test back.

"Hi, Edwin," Bethany goes as I'm turning a corner. I almost go back.

My locker flies open like I never had any trouble with it in my life.

At lunch Hermie's standing there with a tray by himself like he already knew what we wanted.

"Hey there, Herman," Flake says. "Long time no see."

"Hey," Hermie goes.

"What happened to your eye?" Flake goes. "Walk into somebody's boner?"

"No," Hermie goes.

"They got brownies," I tell him.

"I saw," he goes.

"Wanna sit with us?" Flake asks.

Hermie shrugs. While we're standing around looking for a place, Dickhead goes by and dumps an apple core on my tray.

There are no completely empty tables, so we sit with some ninth-grade girls. "Do you mind?" one of them says when Flake's pack leans on her feet under the table.

"Wanna do my hair?" she asks another girl at the table.

"Yeah, maybe in French," the girl tells her.

"So did we tell you we talked to Budzinski?" Flake says to Hermie.

"*He* told me," Hermie goes.

"He do that?" Flake asks, about the black eye. Hermie eats his mac and cheese and looks like he wants to drop the subject.

"Son of a bitch," Flake says, like there'd been some agreement. "I'm gonna talk to that little prick."

"Don't talk to him anymore," Hermie tells him. He touches

his eye with his fingertip and eats more mac and cheese with his other hand.

"Well, he can't just keep beating on you," Flake goes.

"Don't worry about me," Hermie says.

Flake gives me a look. "So listen," he says back. "We got some good news. We'll tell you after school."

"Why can't you tell me now?" Hermie asks.

Flake nods at the girls.

"What do they care?" Hermie wants to know. It's a good question.

Flake holds up his hand like we'll all just have to wait. Hermie gives up and finishes his lunch.

"So what's your good news?" he says after school. He doesn't seem so thrilled just to be hanging out with us.

I haven't talked to Flake since lunch so I don't know. I haven't come up with anything.

He looks at me and sees how much help I'm gonna be. He says to Hermie that we came up with the perfect thing to get even with Budzinski. It's gonna really screw him good.

"What is it?" Hermie wants to know. He doesn't sound excited.

"I don't want to give it away, completely," Flake tells him. "It's pretty complicated to set up."

Hermie just keeps looking at him.

"Anyway, it'll take like two days," Flake goes. "And it has to start on Monday. You in?"

"In what?" Hermie finally says.

"On this thing?" Flake goes. "You wanna get back at him or not?"

"Yeah," Hermie says.

"All right, then," Flake goes.

"That's your good news?" Hermie asks.

"That's our good news," Flake says, frustrated.

"Why's it have to start on Monday?" Hermie asks.

Flake makes a face. "I'll tell you then," he goes.

"Whatever. See you later," Hermie goes. He waves to me and takes off. We watch him walk down the street by himself. He doesn't look up once.

"Shit," Flake says.

"Maybe I'll talk to him again," I go. "I don't think he's gonna do anything."

"Shit," Flake says.

I look at the phone so much after dinner that my dad finally congratulates me on my new hobby. I look at it all night but never call Hermie. Once it's quiet, I go to bed and fall asleep and wake up after twenty minutes. Twenty minutes. I pick up the clock and hold it close to my face because it seems hard to believe.

I leave the light off. I go around the room looking at all the stuff like I'm deciding what to take on a trip. Some stuff it takes a while to figure out with only the light from the window. It's like it becomes itself while I stare at it.

Then I go across the hall and check on Gus. The floor's cold. His foot's sticking out from under the blanket. I stand in my parents' room and look at them. Birds that sing at night make noise outside their window.

I read the newspaper downstairs in the living room with one light on. There's an article on chicken. The front page has a picture of some old guys in suits and ties running from something.

We're going backwards, I realize sitting there. Now even midget sixth-graders think we're assholes.

Back up in bed I watch the ceiling get brighter.

"Good morning," my mom says when I come downstairs.

"Good morning," I go.

"What do you want for breakfast?" she asks.

"The usual," I go. She laughs.

She spends time trying to get me to eat something. I end up with a buttered English muffin on a dish in front of me. I ask for some orange juice, which cheers her up.

"Where's Dad?" I go.

"Office," she goes. "He's got a big lecture he's nervous about. Faculty lecture."

I ask her what a faculty lecture is. It's a lecture for the whole faculty, not just people in economics.

I pick up the English muffin, put it back down again, and drink some orange juice instead. "When is it?" I go.

"Friday," she goes. She pours some beans into the coffee grinder. "I don't know why, but I haven't been feeling like coffee lately."

"Where's Gus?" I go.

"Being a sleepyhead," she goes.

She drops into a seat across the kitchen table and nudges my dish closer to me. "Why do you always pick at your hand like that?" she goes.

"I don't know," I go. I stop doing it.

"So you want to hear my plan?" she asks.

She imitates me, with my mouth open.

"What's your plan?" I ask.

"We go to the beach this weekend," she says. "It's supposed to be in the seventies. The water should still be warm enough for you guys to swim."

"That's a good idea," I tell her.

"You're still sleepy, too," she says.

"What beach?" I ask.

"That one *you* like," she tells me.

"By Grandma's old place?" I go.

"That's the one," she goes.

"It takes like four hours to get there," I go.

She holds my hand and turns it over and looks at the palm. "This is part of the surprise," she goes. "I say we pick your father up and we're all ready to go right after his lecture. Let 'im throw his tweed jacket in the trunk."

"When's his lecture over?" I go.

"Ten or so," she goes. "It's reading period."

Little areas of my head feel cold, then tingly. "*This* Friday?" I go. "I got school."

"We'll take you out early," she goes. "Get Out of Jail Free."

"Unless you're dying to stay in school," she says when I don't say anything.

Gus calls down the stairs, wanting to know where his sippy cup is.

"I don't know, hon," she calls back up to him. "What'd you do with it?"

I should say I have a test. Or *some*thing. My shoulders start bobbing like I'm using them to think.

"You're gonna be late," she goes. She tips her head at the clock. When Gus calls her again I get my pack and go.

When I see Flake I tell him that my mom wants to take me out of school on Friday to go to the beach. He nods. He's excited because he had the idea of scratching *You're Next* on the mirror in the boys' bathroom. He did it with a roofing nail. He says it looks cool. "Check it out," he goes. "It creeps you out. You look at your face and that's what's written over it."

It would creep me out, I tell him.

"So you talk to Hermie?" he goes.

He doesn't look fazed when I shake my head.

"I don't think he'll do anything before Friday," he says. "If he does anything at all."

The bell for homeroom rings but neither of us gets up off the step for a minute. The sky's a nice blue and there's a breeze.

Off on the monkey bars a squirrel's sitting on his hind legs and has his head up like he's sunning his face.

Nobody seems like they're in a hurry.

Weensie's in our way on the stairs. "Hey," he says to me, before going up ahead of us.

"What was *that* about?" Flake asks.

"You got me," I tell him.

Before third period I go look at Flake's *You're Next* on the mirror. It does look cool. But while I'm washing my hands in front of it, a kid comes and goes without even noticing it.

When I come out of the bathroom, Tawanda waves me over. She's with a group of black girls who think the whole thing's funny. They stand there talking trash to each other while I walk over.

"Michelle talk to you?" she goes.

"About what?" I go.

"Ms. Arnold talk to you?" she goes.

"Nobody talks to me," I tell her.

"You don't *have* conversations," one of the black girls says.

"I don't have conversations," I go.

"*I'm* talking to you," Tawanda goes.

"*She's* talking to you," the black girl says.

I wish I could think of something funny to say back. "Uh," I end up saying.

"So turns out Ms. Arnold *loves* our World of Color thing," Tawanda says.

"Yeah, she said," I go.

"So you *did* talk to her," Tawanda goes.

"She said it a while ago," I tell her.

"No, she *really* loves it," Tawanda goes. "She's entering it in the regional fair for the art prize."

"The tree with the heads in it?" I ask. Some of the black girls laugh.

"She wants to call it *The Fruit of Human Endeavor*," Tawanda goes.

"I know," she goes when she sees my expression. "They always do something queer at the last second so you can't enjoy it."

A small kid walks on his knees from one classroom across the hall to the other. We all watch.

"This is a weird fucking school," one of the other black girls says.

"She said she especially liked the heads with the helmets and the Fish-Man head," Tawanda tells me.

"*I* did those heads," I go.

"I know," Tawanda goes. "That's why I'm telling you. You're a star."

The other girls are talking to each other by this point.

"Thanks for telling me," I go.

"No problem," she goes.

"See you," I go.

"So I don't wanna hear about you working with other people," she tells me. "On projects. Just remember who knew you when."

"C'mon," I go, and she turns back to the other girls. All through third period I'm surprised to find myself smiling about it.

Ms. Arnold catches me in the hall before lunch and says that if we win the regional prize, I get my name in the paper. "You ever wonder what it'd be like to see your name in the paper?" she asks.

"Yeah," I go.

"Did you ever think it might happen?" she asks.

"Yeah," I go.

She smiles, like she wasn't expecting that. "Well, you tell your parents," she goes. "It's already a big honor, you know, just to get this far."

"I know," I tell her.

"It's great that it was a cooperative project, too," she goes.

"I guess," I go.

She seems like she wants to say something else. If she does, she doesn't say it. She runs her fingernail along the edge of her lipstick.

"Well, thanks again," I tell her.

She puts her hand up to my cheek, just like I imagined Bethany doing it.

"Edwin Hanratty," she says, like I was a place she used to love to visit. "What a strange little guy you are."

"What happened to *you?*" Flake says when he sees me in the lunch line. "Why're you holding your cheek?"

In social studies they're doing the Anasazis. When the period's over I have one sentence written in my notebook: "The Anasazis had their own religion, but it wasn't that complex."

After school I don't take the bus and look for Flake instead. When I see him he's already a block down the street. I call him and he stops and scratches his head so hard I can hear it from where I am.

"What're you doing?" I ask when I catch up.

"I gotta lot of things to do to get ready," he goes.

"*You* gotta lot of things to do?" I go.

"Yeah. I gotta lot of things to do," he goes.

I stop walking. He keeps going. *Well, fuck you, too*, I think.

By the time I get back to the parking lot, the buses are gone. I end up walking home.

There's a note on the counter that Gus has an ear infection and my mom's taking him to the doctor. My dad must be off working on his lecture. I have to get out of the house. I change into shorts to save my pants. I hold the pants up after taking them off and can see my hand where the butt's starting to wear through.

I have skinny legs.

I go out the back door and wander over to our mosh-volleyball court. I don't see the volleyball in the garage.

The sun goes in and it's cooler out. Gus's Nerf football is at the end of the driveway. I pick it up to wing it back into the yard, but then keep it. I walk toward the JV practice fields like I'm heading for a big pickup Nerf game. I try to hit squirrels or birds with ambush lobs on the way.

The practice fields are empty. I don't know why. I climb the fence and sit on the grass with the Nerf. A pigeon wanders by out of range.

A tan dog with floppy ears and white paws is sniffing and taking a dump in the middle of the field. I can't tell what kind it is.

A kid a little older than Gus who's wearing a towel like a cape comes through the gate at the other end. He has a Styro-foam glider. His dad trails after him, dragging a knapsack. The kid's hair is short on the sides and sticks out on top like a patch of dandelions. He throws the glider a few times straight into the ground and then gives up. He heads over to me and his dad gets the glider and takes it apart and puts the pieces into the knapsack.

The kid stops a little ways away. He's got his eye on the Nerf. "Throw," he goes.

The dad comes up behind him. He's got an expression like he just found out I screwed him over.

"Throw," the kid goes.

"Am I gonna have to worry about your dog?" the guy says.

"Throw," the kid goes.

"Are you deaf?" the guy says.

"No," I go.

"So do I have to worry about your dog?" he says.

"No," I go.

He looks over at the dog like I'm not very reassuring. The dog looks at him. "Get outta here," he says to the dog, though it wasn't heading towards him.

"Throw," the kid goes.

I throw him the Nerf. He fumbles around with it for a while. His towel gets in the way. He kicks the ball back and forth. He runs with it under his arm. He asks his dad to catch it. His dad drags the knapsack farther away from me and then lets it go and puts his arms out. The kid can't throw at all.

The dad troops after it all over the field and then the kid picks it up and stuffs it in the knapsack. He pulls his glider out and his dad puts it back together for him and the kid throws it into the ground for a while. Then he says something and his dad picks up the pack and the glider and they both head for the gate across the field.

"Hey," I go. They keep walking. *"Hey,"* I call. I get up and follow them. *"Hey!"*

The dad turns around. The kid keeps going.

"You got my ball," I go.

"What?" the dad says.

"The Nerf ball," I tell him.

"That's his," the dad goes. "We brought it here." He waits for me to say something and then starts walking again.

"I don't fucking believe this," I go.

He turns around again. "What'd you say?" he goes. He walks back towards me. "What did you say to me?"

"That's my ball," I go.

"What did you *say* to me?" he goes.

"I said I don't fucking believe this," I tell him.

He gives me a two-handed shove and I go flying.

"You're just gonna steal my fucking *ball*?" I yell when I get up.

He comes at me again and I take off. When I get a little

ways away, I yell back at him, "It's not even *mine*. It's my little *brother's*."

They keep walking. The kid looks like he's asking his father something. His towel's covering his back and trailing in the grass.

"You hear me, you *fuck*?" I scream.

They keep walking.

I run after them, to follow them home and break every fucking window in their house. But they get into a station wagon outside the gate and drive away. I try to read the license plate and then fall on my butt after they take the corner. I wipe my eyes and kick my feet out, like I'm having a tantrum.

What were you gonna do? I think to myself. Report them to Motor Vehicles?

12

"You're eating again," my dad says to me at dinner. "He's eating again," he tells my mother when I don't say anything.

"I see that," my mom tells him back. She's made pork chops and a salad and I'm even eating the salad.

"I'm eating, too," Gus volunteers.

"So you are," my dad tells him.

"So you almost finished?" my mom asks my dad. Gus spills his milk. My dad lifts his plate and my mom goes to get a sponge.

"Maybe I picked the wrong topic," he says. "Who really cares about the World Bank?" He turns to me. "You care about the World Bank?"

"Not right this second," I tell him.

"There you have it," my dad says.

"Well, Edwin's going to be in school," my mom tells him. She finishes mopping the table and squeezes the sponge out in the sink. "So he's not going to be able to make it anyway."

My dad puts his plate back down. "What's the matter with you?" he asks me.

"What do you mean?" I go.

"You're making little noises," he says.

"I am?" I go.

He imitates one.

"I'm doing that?" I ask.

My mom nods. Gus makes the sound, too.

"Something on your mind?" my dad asks.

"I don't know," I tell him.

"The old glass head," he goes.

I put my elbows on the sides of my dish and hold my head steady with my hands. I don't look at either of them, or at Gus.

"After dinner, you have to have your medicine," my mom reminds Gus.

"No," Gus goes.

"Is that for his ear?" I ask, and she nods.

Gus complains for a while and we all finish eating.

"So you don't want to talk about what's bothering you?" my dad asks me.

"Maybe in a little while," I tell him.

"Mom?" Gus asks.

"Something at school?" my mom asks me. She's got her back to me because she's carried her dish to the sink.

"I don't know," I tell her. "We'll see."

"Mom?" Gus asks.

She looks over her shoulder at me and makes an exaggerated disappointed face. My dad gets a pencil from the counter and writes some notes on his paper napkin.

"I think your father's working too hard," my mom says to me when she comes back to the table.

"Hard but not well," my dad goes. He draws a line on his napkin from one note to another.

"Mom?" Gus asks.

"Your ear hurt?" I ask him.

"Yeah," he goes. He tilts his head and puts his hand on it. His hand's still holding his fork.

"You're getting pork in your hair," my mom goes. She clears my plate, and my dad's.

Gus has to finish before he gets dessert. I sit upstairs on my bed with my hands back on the sides of my face. I can hear my dad talking to himself in the downstairs bathroom. "Nobody flushes in this house," he says. Gus is singing to himself instead of eating. His new favorite song is "I've Got the Whole World in My Pants."

He quiets down. My dad turns on the TV. Down the street a dog starts doing the same bark for ten minutes in a row.

I find myself squatting over by the bookcase. I stopped flipping through the serial-killers book when I got to the picture of Richard Speck. He doesn't look like anybody I know.

"Where'd you *get* that book?" my mom asks from over my shoulder. She smiles when I jump. I didn't hear her come in. "I can't believe they *have* books like that for kids," she says.

"It's not for kids," I tell her.

"That's for sure," she says. She puts away some laundry she's folded in my drawer and picks up my green pants. "These are about ready to go out, aren't they?" she asks.

"Leave them," I tell her.

"We can try to find you a new pair like these," she says.

"They're okay," I tell her.

She drops them and holds up her hands like I've gotten all bent out of shape. "Why're you *crying*?" she asks. She kneels down next to me. "What's *wrong*?"

"I bit my tongue," I tell her.

She wants to see, so I open my mouth. "I don't see it," she says.

"It's on the bottom," I go. I can't tell whether she believes me or not. She gets to her feet and watches me for a minute, then picks up the laundry basket and heads downstairs. I hear her saying something to my dad.

I lie down and slide under the bed. I push my hands against the planks holding up the box spring. I hear Gus get halfway up the stairs and then stop. "Where's my ball?" he asks somebody.

"What?" my mom says. She's in the TV room with my dad.

"Where's my Nerf ball?" Gus goes.

"I think you left it outside," she tells him.

"I want it," he goes.

"Didn't you leave it outside?" she asks.

"I want it," he goes.

"Well, we can't get it now," she tells him. "We'll get it tomorrow."

He's quiet a minute and then keeps coming upstairs. I can see his feet inside my room. "Edwin?" he says.

He goes back downstairs. "Where's Edwin?" he asks.

"He's up in his room," my mom tells him.

He comes back upstairs. "Edwin?" he calls.

I'm crying again. *"Edwin?"* he calls.

"I'm under here," I tell him.

He gets down on his hands and knees and looks under the bed. He laughs and crawls under with me. He's small enough to slide up next to me and roll over on his back. "Are we hiding?" he asks.

"Yeah," I tell him. We lie like that until my mom comes up to put him to bed.

"Are we sleeping *under* the bed tonight?" she asks after she sings him his song and shuts his door. Now I can see her feet where his were. She's wearing her poofy slippers. "Edwin?" she asks.

"I'm just lying here a minute," I go.

Her feet turn and the bed creaks when she sits on it. The box spring sags closer. "Can I ask you a question?" she asks.

"Uh-huh," I go.

"What's wrong?" she asks.

"Nothing," I go.

"I'm talking to a bed, here," she goes. "So *some*thing's wrong."

I'm crying again. I wipe my face so hard it hurts.

"Edwin?" she goes. I try not to make any noise. She gets off the bed and gets on her hands and knees and lowers her head so she can see. "What's the *matter?*" she asks. Honey?"

I wish I were Gus. "I hurt my face," I tell her.

"What'd you do?" she asks. She reaches a hand under and touches it.

"Rubbed it too hard," I tell her.

"Oh, Edwin," she goes.

I slide out and sit up next to her. *Tell* her about it, the baby part of me goes. I can just imagine Flake's face. "Oh, Ma," I go.

She hugs me. "It's okay," she goes.

"What is?" I go.

"Whatever it is," she says. She rubs circles on my back. "Sometimes we can't handle stuff," she tells me. "Sometimes it's just too much."

"I can handle anything," I tell her.

"Well, don't get mad," she says. "What're you getting mad for?"

"I'm gonna take a shower," I go. I get up.

"Wait. What're you getting mad about?" she says.

"Thanks," I go.

"Honey, you're just a little guy," she tells me. "Don't take everything so hard."

"*Wait,*" she says.

I shut the bathroom door behind me and turn the shower on.

"*Shit,*" she says.

She finally asks through the bathroom door if we can talk tomorrow, and when I say yes she goes downstairs. I turn off the shower and listen. After I'm sure she's not coming back I dry off and climb into bed naked. I get a hard-on. "I don't know what you think *you're* doing," I say to it.

I'm still sniffing and crying. I can't even stay in bed. It feels like there are bugs in it. Every time I pull the sheets down and turn on the lights, there's nothing there. I take another shower. I sit in the tub and let the water pound my head until it starts to get cold and I have to turn it off.

I have these weird, dozy, half-dreams sitting in my chair. In one I'm a cowboy. When I remember it it's a little embarrassing I made myself a cowboy.

I go to the window. Down the street, a few lights are still on. What will it be like on Saturday? Or a week from Saturday?

I walk all over the room. Sometimes I get down in a squat and press my hands together until they shake. Then I get up again and keep walking.

I grab the phone and dial the first three numbers of our number and then anything, any other four numbers. An answering machine picks up. "Welcome to Target World," I go after the beep, and then I hang up.

It's no fun, though, so I don't do it again.

I go back to the chair. I go back under the bed. *This is unreal,* I think. *This is un-real.* But then I think that when people say something's unreal, they just mean it's too real.

"Your brother's upset," my mom says at breakfast. Gus is crying in the bathroom.

"About what?" I go.

"He can't find his ball," she says. "You seen it?"

I nod. "I'll find it," I go. I'll buy him another one, I figure. They have them at the drugstore, and I can ride my bike there.

"Nice way to start the day," my dad says, sitting down next to me. Gus hears him and starts wailing.

"Don't make fun of him," my mom tells him.

"I'm not making fun of him," my dad goes. "I'm just commenting on our happy home." She pours him some coffee. "Did he look outside?" he asks.

"He says he looked all over," my mom tells him.

"I looked *all over*," Gus says from the bathroom.

"And how are *you* today?" my dad asks me.

"I'm good," I tell him.

"You *look* great," he tells me back.

"I think I know where his ball is," I tell my mom.

"Well, tell him that," she says. She walks over to the bathroom door. "Honey? Edwin says he knows where your ball is."

"Where?" Gus wails.

"You'll have to ask him, honey," she goes. She comes back into the kitchen.

The bathroom door opens and Gus walks into the room. "You got it?" he asks.

"I think maybe Flake borrowed it," I go. "I'll get it from him."

"*Flake* has it?" my dad asks.

"I *think* Flake borrowed it," I go. "I'll get it back," I tell Gus. "I promise."

"Now?" Gus asks.

"Not now," I go. I'm so tired it's like I can't see. "When I come home from school."

I finally get my books out of my locker before homeroom and somebody pokes me under the arm and tips them all over the floor.

"Congratulations," Michelle says when I turn around. "I *told* you it was a great idea."

"It wasn't your *idea*," Tawanda tells her. "It was how he did it."

I assume they mean the tree with the heads. I start collecting books off the floor, and Dickhead goes by and golfs a paperback with his foot all the way down the hall. A few seventh-grade girls twist to avoid it as it sails by.

"What an asshole," Michelle says, but when he turns on her she looks thrilled.

"What're you gonna do about it?" he says to me.

"Oh, I got something in mind," I go. I collect my other books and stand up.

"You got something in mind?" he goes.

"Mr. Lopez," the vice principal says to him. "Come with me."

Michelle and Tawanda make gloating noises. "Where you going, Edwin?" Tawanda says to me. "Don't you be a stranger," she calls when I'm almost at the other end of the hall, and Michelle laughs. "I got *plans* for you."

Before third period I pass the gym. I pass the side door where we're going to jam the wedge.

Before fourth period outside of math there's a group of kids standing around laughing and making a lot of noise about a piece of paper. "Make Edwin take it," one kid goes when I walk up. I can't even get into the room.

This fat kid gets out of the way and Bethany's behind him. "Here, Edwin," she goes. She hands me a different piece of paper that's folded into a thick triangle. On the outside somebody's written *Sex Test*.

"Fischetti has the lowest score so far," some kid behind her says.

"Let *me* see that," Flake goes. He walks over from across the hall.

"No, no," the fat kid says. "Don't let him see it."

Flake holds out his hand. Bethany smiles at him. "Roddy, tell Edwin we need him to fill this out," she goes.

He looks at me like this is my fault.

"Hey, *I* don't wanna do this," I tell him.

He walks away. "Hey," I call after him. The bell rings.

Bethany puts her hand on the sex test in my hand and leans closer. "This is for science," she goes, and her friends laugh. Everybody heads to their classes. Some kids have to run.

We both go into math. I leave the sex test on my desk throughout the period. I don't open it. The teacher comes down the aisle while somebody's putting a problem on the board and scoops it up and looks at the title, then throws it in his wastebasket when he gets back to the front of the room.

Ms. Meier finds me in the lunchroom and hands me my copy of *A Separate Peace*. I left it in her classroom and apparently need it for the assignment tonight.

"How'd you know it was mine?" I ask her. I don't remember writing my name in it.

"Who else would cross out the *A* and write *No* over it?" she goes.

"Mr. Hanratty," the vice principal says, when I come out of the lunch line with my tray. "A minute of your time."

"Now?" I go.

"You can eat while we talk," he says.

We sit at a table full of sixth-graders, including Budzinski. He keeps his eye on us the whole time. I feel like making a gesture toward him, like we're talking about him.

"I didn't do anything," I go. "I was just picking up my books and he kicked one down the hall."

"Oh, this isn't about Mr. Lopez," the vice principal goes.

I offer him a boiled carrot.

He chuckles. "We'll be sending a note home as well, but I

just wanted to remind you that you're going to be starting that socialization workshop next week," he goes.

"Oh, God," I go. I put down my Salisbury steak.

"It's not going to be that bad," he goes.

"When?" I go.

"It's not going to be that *bad*," he goes. "You need to give it a chance."

"Oh, God," I go.

"Give it a chance," he tells me.

I push my tray away. I can't be in school one more minute. "Who else is in it?" I ask him.

He tells me. It's even worse than I thought. Dickhead, Weensie, Hogan. Two girls I never heard of. Another kid I heard bit the head off a parrot.

"It's after school," he goes. "So you won't miss any class time."

"Oh, good," I go.

"The feeling is that you can't go on like this," he tells me. "That something radical needs to happen."

"I think you're right," I tell him back. I'm tearing up again. In front of him. In front of the lunchroom. "I think you're right."

I go to the nurse's office. Another headache. I start throwing up, too. During sixth period there's a knock on the door of the little room where they put me, and when I pull the facecloth off my eyes, Ms. Arnold pokes her head in and comes over to my cot.

"What's the class doing?" I ask her.

"I gave them an assignment," she says. She puts her hand on my leg. "Are you okay, Edwin?"

"I got sick," I tell her.

"I see that," she says. She smiles the way she did before. I think about her touching my cheek. I start to get a hard-on and pull a knee up to hide it. This is unbelievable.

"Is your stomach bothering you?" she asks.

"Why're you visiting me?" I ask her back. She's the last person I want there. When she touches me again I jump.

"Sorry," she says. She looks embarrassed. "I was looking through your portfolio," she finally adds.

We keep them in the room, in long narrow cubbies.

"I found the one you called *Mental*," she says.

"So?" I go.

"Want to tell me about it?" she asks.

"You saw it," I go.

"How long'd it take you to do it?" she asks.

"I don't know," I go.

"It's quite a piece," she says.

It's a big sheet and I filled it with half-inch marks. Sometimes the marks went through the paper. I did it to count minutes the way guys in prison count days. I kept it underneath other things I was working on. By the end it looked black, when you stepped back. There's like eight million half-inch marks on it. I wrote *Mental* at the top of it as a joke, after Tawanda saw it.

"You mind if I show it to some other people?" she asks.

"Like who?" I go.

"Oh, I don't know," she says. "Like Mr. Davis. Maybe Mrs. Pruitt."

"I just saw him at lunch," I go. I close my eyes. I'm so tired. I spread out again on the cot. Big see-through plates bang around behind my eyelids.

"I'll let you rest," I hear her say. Then the door shuts behind her.

"Don't call me, I'll call you," Flake goes when the buses are getting ready to pull out. He's holding out his two bandaged fingers and flexing them, like he's getting ready for action.

"More stuff to do, huh?" I go.

He heads off without answering. That's all right with me. When I get home I get five dollars from my money dish and bike to the drugstore. They have Gus's football but in a different color. I ask the guy and of course they don't have one with his color in the back. I go back and forth about it. "Hey, kid, it's a Nerf ball," the guy finally goes. "You're not picking a college here."

When I ride back up the driveway Gus is playing in a scuffed-up area around some tree roots. He's got a metal airplane without wings and he's swooping it around and crashing it into the roots. "You get my ball?" he goes.

I pull it out of the cardboard inside my knapsack and hand it over. He looks at it. His was purple. This one's pink.

"This one's pink," he goes.

"Yours was pink," I go.

"Mine was pink?" he goes.

"Yours was pink," I go.

"Mine wasn't pink," I hear him go as I head into the house.

"Oh boy, is your dad having a bad day," my mom goes when I pass through the kitchen.

Gus follows me in. "Mine wasn't pink," he tells my mom while I head upstairs.

"What, honey?" my mom asks. I shut my door.

I sit on the bed. By this time tomorrow everything will be different. Everything will be over. It doesn't feel like that.

I have to get stuff together. I have to get organized. I don't even know what to organize. I should make a list, I think. I pull a piece of paper and a pencil off my desk and write on my thigh. I write: *List:*

"Was his ball pink?" my mom calls up the stairs. "He says it wasn't."

"It was," I call back down. "He's losing his mind."

"He says it was, honey," I hear her tell Gus in a low voice.

He starts whining. "I *like* the pink," I hear her say. "You don't like the pink?"

"Jesus God Almighty in Heaven," my dad says from his room. He must have his laptop in there.

I can't sit still. I get off the bed, walk around the room, sit on the bed again.

I call Flake. His mom says he's out. "Hold on," she says. "He just came in."

"You're blowing me off?" I say when he gets on the phone.

"What do you want?" he goes.

"I wanted to know if you wanted to come over," I tell him. I look out my window. Gus is booting the Nerf around the back. Over in our neighbor's yard their golden retriever is standing at their fence, watching him like he's dinner.

"Maybe we could have one more game of mosh volleyball," I go.

"Mosh volleyball," he goes, like he'll never do that again. Then I think he probably won't.

"You all right?" he asks. "You're panting. You sound like a dog."

"I'm scared," I finally tell him.

He's quiet a second. "Don't wuss out on me," he goes. " You hear me?"

"I'm not wussing out on anybody," I go.

"Are you *crying*?" he goes.

"No," I go.

"Jesus," he goes.

"What?" I go. My mom comes up the stairs and into my room. She sits on the bed and puts a hand on my side.

"Are you gonna make it?" he goes. "Do I have to come over there and sit with you?"

"No," I go. "I just wanted to see if you wanted to play volley-ball, that's all." I look at my mom. She looks sympathetic.

"We got a lot to do tonight," he goes. "How soon can you come over after everybody's asleep there?"

My mom still has her hand on my side. She smoothes it up and down like she's rubbing a dog's coat.

"I don't know," I go.

"One? One-thirty?" he goes.

"Yeah," I go.

"Which?" he goes. "One?"

"No," I go.

"One-thirty?" he goes.

"Yeah," I go.

"All right. Come to the garage," he tells me. "Don't forget your stuff for the capsule."

"The what?" I go.

"The thing we're gonna bury," he goes.

My mom smiles at me. She notices the piece of paper with *List:* on it and smiles again.

"You gonna be all right?" he goes.

"Yeah," I go. He hangs up.

"You having a fight with Roddy?" my mom asks when I hang up.

"Sort of," I go.

"It'll be all right," she says.

"Thanks," I go.

She gets off the bed and opens my dresser drawers.

"What're you doing here?" I ask her.

"I'm helping you pack for tomorrow," she tells me.

Around midnight Gus has a bad dream. I creep out of bed with my clothes on and stand by his door.

"E*dwin*," he moans.

I wait, in case he's going to wake up. I go back to my room

and get under the covers in case my mom comes up to check on him. He doesn't make any more noise. Across the room on my chair is the little suitcase she packed for the beach.

At one-twenty I go down to the living room and listen. The stairs make noise but my mom and dad don't. I give it a minute and then leave.

There's nobody on the streets. *Suppose you disappeared?* a voice goes. *Suppose you never made it to his house?* My sneakers make rubbery noises on the pavement the whole way over.

"In here," Flake says, in one of those whispers you can hear a block away when I turn into his driveway. He's standing in the garage in the dark.

"What're you doing with a hockey stick?" I ask when my eyes get used to the dark.

"My dad's taping up his team's sticks," he goes, like that answers my question. He puts the edge of the stick under my chin and flips it up.

"*Ow,*" I go.

"Shhh," he goes.

"What're you *doing?*" I go. I'm holding my chin with one hand.

"Imagine when a real hockey player does it," he goes. I hear the clunk when he sets it back against the wall with the others. The dog next door starts barking even though he's in the house.

"Asshole dog," Flake says to himself.

He leads me into the house. At the back door he turns and puts his finger to his mouth, like otherwise I'd go in talking. On the stairs we try to walk together so it sounds like one person.

We're halfway up when his father goes, "Roddy?"

We both freeze.

"Yeah?" Flake goes.

"What're you doing?" his dad goes.

"Getting some water," he goes.

"The water upstairs no good?" his dad goes.

We look at each other. "It doesn't get cold enough," Flake tells him.

We don't hear anything for a minute.

"Don't get up again," his dad finally says.

After we shut the door and turn on his desk lamp he widens his eyes and tilts his head, like, that was close.

He's got the gun duffels from inside the cases under the bed. He pulls out the edge of one to show me. Then we sit facing each other on the blanket without saying anything. He watches the clock. I get sad thinking about the little suitcase my mom left on the chair.

When he's satisfied with the time, he gets on his hands and knees and pulls out the duffels and zips them open. We start with mine. I show him I can release the safety.

"The clip release is this thing here," he whispers.

"How'd you get them out of your dad's closet?" I whisper back. "Aren't you worried he's gonna see they're missing?"

He shakes his head. "I locked the cases back up," he says. "I left the pistol."

The release is a black metal thing in front of the trigger and behind the clip. Neither of us can work it.

"You're supposed to use your thumb," he goes.

"I'm using my thumb," I tell him.

He takes the gun out of my hands and braces the stock against his belly and works his thumb up under the thing. It's hard with his bandaged fingers. There's like a flange that's bent at a right angle. That's the release.

"When're those going to come off?" I go, meaning the bandages.

"The guy said he'd look at them next Thursday," he goes. He wedges one thumb behind the other and pushes.

"I think they made this with a pair of pliers," I tell him.

"Well, the Russians. You know," he says. He turns it to try to get more leverage.

"No, I don't know," I go. "I don't know any Russians."

"Ha ha," he goes, and there's a snap and the clip falls onto the bed.

We snap it back in and try it again. We pretty much get the hang of it.

"How much is in a clip?" I go.

He peers inside one.

"You can't tell like that," I go.

"When did you become the expert on automatic weapons?" he goes.

"I know that much," I go.

"Shhh," he goes.

I ask how we're going to carry the extra clips. It turns out that his plan is to have them in the duffels with the guns in our lockers.

"You got pants with pockets big enough to hold a few of these?" he asks.

"I don't know. Cargo shorts," I tell him.

"There you go," he says.

I measure the clip width with my finger and thumb and try to remember how wide the pockets are. I heft the gun. "This is heavy," I tell him.

"Yeah, it's really heavy. Hold it farther up with that hand," he tells me.

I swing it back and forth around the room without the clip in it.

"Wanna trade?" he asks.

"Lemme see yours," I go, and he hands over the carbine. It feels much lighter. "Maybe," I go.

"Well, decide," he goes. "I don't want us arguing about this tomorrow."

I take the Kalashnikov in one hand and the carbine in the other. I can't decide. I start sweating all at once. "I can't believe we're really going to do this," I go.

"I know," he goes. He locks a clip into the carbine and then ejects it. He sights down the barrel and then lays the gun down on the bed. "You want a Go-Gurt?" he goes. "I brought two up." I shake my head. He tears off the corner of a Go-Gurt and sucks on it. We have to stay close on the bed so we can hear each other whispering.

"We'll probably shoot all the wrong people," I go. I try to make it sound like a joke.

He slurps his Go-Gurt and lays his hand on the barrel of the Kalashnikov.

"You worry about that?" I go.

He does his constipated-monkey thing. *Inka inka inka inka.*

"Guess you don't," I go.

"Oh, I almost forgot," he says. He pulls out two packages of little rubber plugs. "Earplugs. My dad says you can't believe how loud they are."

He wants to play something from his *Great Speeches* CD that he says will psych us up, but he has to keep it turned down so low that I can't make out what the guy's saying even when we have our ears right up to the speakers. He keeps asking if I can hear it and finally gets mad and turns it off.

"You know what *I* think about?" he says once we're back up on the bed.

There's a noise downstairs. We both stop.

After a minute, we gather all the clips and slide them into the duffels, then angle the guns in after them and slide both duffels under the bed.

We listen again. A car goes by.

"You know what *I* think about?" he asks again.

I shake my head.

He rubs his face. "The way when something terrible happens somewhere there's all these flags and flowers and candles, pictures of the people who died and pages of sayings and poems. I don't think about my picture in the papers or on TV. I think about that stuff." He's looking down at his crotch. "What're you looking at my dick for?" he goes.

"That's where *you* were looking," I go.

"You ever think about stuff like that?" he goes. "All those flowers and shit lined up for months and months?"

I shrug. "I guess," I go.

He gives me a look.

The look gets me pissed off. *Why am I always the pussy?* I think.

"Let's do it," he tells me.

It's easier if we put one duffel on top of the other and grab both handles. It takes us about a block and a half to figure this out. We lug the things along worrying about cars, but we only see one that's heading in the wrong direction.

We circle the school out in the athletic fields to avoid the lights on the building, then hustle the bags over to the back stairs and dump them underneath where it's dark. We both stand around with our hands on our thighs, breathing hard.

I can hear Flake feeling around in the dark. "They never *fixed* this?" he goes. The window opens and I hear him sliding through.

He calls for the bags. I pull them over and he drags them through. When I climb in I forget how far the drop is and lose my balance and knock him over against the bags.

"It's all right," he goes.

The corridors are narrow so we each have to carry our own. We put them on our backs and hunch over while we walk. We sling the handles over our shoulders. He gets out his little flashlight and holds it in his teeth. We go through some doors and then up the stairs. The door at the top is locked.

He sits down. He's still got the flashlight in his teeth, and it's shining on part of the stair railing.

"What do we do now?" I go.

He sits there. A minute goes by.

"Remember that guy in the SUV?" he goes.

It takes me a second to figure out who he's talking about. Plus it's hard to understand him with the flashlight in his mouth. "The old guy?" I go.

"Yeah," he goes. When he nods the light slides up and down the railing. "The guy that followed us."

The cement's cold on my butt. He's waiting for me to say something. "I know who you mean," I tell him.

"He followed me again last week," he goes. "At like four in the morning."

I slide my duffel around so it's not hurting my hip. "What were you doing out?" I go.

He ignores the question. "I got in his car," he goes. I can see him watching me. "He gave me a blow job." The light in his mouth moves a little. "You hear me?"

"Yeah," I go. "Why'd you let him?"

He shrugs. "I wanted to know what it felt like." Then he gets up and hoists the duffel higher on his back. "Come on."

"Where're we going?" I whisper.

We go back down the stairs and along some corridors and turn a different way. That leads to another locked door. We turn back and go up some other stairs. The duffels are heavy.

At the top there's another door. He hesitates, and then puts his hand on it. It opens. "The door down to the art storeroom," he goes. "I figured they'd leave it open."

It's two hallways to Flake's locker. He opens it and stuffs the duffel in standing up. It barely fits and we have to tuck in part of it so it doesn't catch on the door. The next hallway over we find mine. Flake holds the flashlight while I work the combination. Of course I can't get it to open.

"Gimme that," he finally says. "What's the combination?"

It works on the first try for him. We go back out the way we came.

We don't talk until we're off school property. "You forgot your shit for us to bury," he tells me.

"Yeah," I go.

"I won't bury mine, then, either," he goes after a minute. "They'll find it anyway."

When I get home I stand outside my house in the front yard and look at it. The moon's out. The trees make black patterns over one side with their shadows.

It's four o'clock. I think about Flake in the car with the old guy.

I head down my driveway. My sneakers are still making those rubbery sounds on the pavement. I look at our bushes. I look at the garage. I look at our mosh-volleyball court.

I stand in the back porch for a minute, getting used to the indoor darkness. My feet are wet from the grass. I get a drink of water and go upstairs. I stand around in the upstairs hallway and then peep into Gus's room. He's on his back with a hand above his head. He's holding his new Nerf against his side with the other hand.

I put a finger near his face on the pillow. When I go to leave, he says, "What're you doing?"

"Shhh," I tell him. I come back to the bed and get down on one knee beside his head.

"Is it dark out?" he wants to know.

"Yeah, it's still dark," I whisper.

"Is Mommy up?" he goes.

"Mommy's sleeping," I go.

"What're you doing?" he goes.

"I'm just going to sleep," I tell him. "You go to sleep, too." I pull the covers up to his chest. "You like your Nerf ball?" I go.

"Yeah," he goes.

"This one's pink," he tells me.

I clear my throat. One of his shoes is on the windowsill for some reason.

"Don't be sad," he tells me.

"That's what everybody says," I go. "Why does everybody say that?"

"I don't know," he says.

"I just get so *mad* sometimes," I tell him. I get mad just thinking about it. I make a fist and push it as hard as I can into my hip.

He holds up his ball and I tuck it back under the covers. "How's your ear?" I go.

"It hurts," he says.

"Does it hurt now?" I ask him.

"No," he says.

We don't say anything for a few minutes. He rolls onto his side. He's starting to get drowsy again.

"Okay, go to sleep now," I whisper.

"Good night," he goes.

"Good night," I go. "You're a great little guy, you know that?"

"Yeah," he goes. "But leave the door open," he goes.

For the first time in however long my mom has to wake me up for school. "Let's *go*," she says. I have no idea how long she's been in my room.

While I get dressed she strips the bed and talks about when

she's going to come get me. She has errands to run so she won't get there till a quarter of twelve or so.

I sit on the floor and pull on my cargo shorts. Assembly's at eleven.

"You're not wearing your pants," she says.

I had my clothes all arranged in order so I could get them on faster.

I look at her and she looks at me. Something goes across her expression. She twists the sheets together and lifts them up and carries them down the stairs.

I forget my earplugs and have to go back up to my room.

Everything I eat and drink feels like it stays up in my throat. "Your brother's conked out this morning, too," my mom goes. She's making and wrapping sandwiches to eat on the road. She reminds me not to forget to show my homeroom teacher the note. "And be where I said," she tells me. "Don't make us come looking all over the building for you."

"I won't," I go. "Where's Dad?"

"He went in early to practice his thing," she tells me.

"Tell him I said good luck," I go.

"You're going to be late," she says.

I stop at the door but she's already gone down to the basement with a load of laundry.

At the bus stop the ninth-graders are having a loogie contest. One kid hawks one way farther than anybody else, and it lands on my pack. "Hey," I go.

"*Hey*," the kid goes. The other kids laugh.

I don't have anything to wipe it off with. I end up dragging it along the grass and it just smears around.

"*Hey*," the kid goes. The whole ride they keep saying it to each other—"*Hey*"—and then they all laugh.

I wait by myself on the playground before homeroom. Flake stays away from me.

When the bell rings I go sit in my chair and look at the pinecone on my homeroom teacher's desk. It's next to her water bottle. Some kids are whispering during announcements, and a girl in front of me goes, "Oh my God, *what* is so funny?"

Assembly's fourth period, so I'll be getting out of math. My foot keeps bouncing on the floor under my desk.

In English they're diagramming sentences. Ms. Meier calls on me to go up to the board three straight times, and even though I didn't do the homework I get all three sentences right. After the third one, a girl goes, "Edwin's on a *roll*," and Michelle goes, "I swear, there's someone in his brain *doing* this for him."

When I sit back down, my hands are shaking. Ms. Meier tells me I'm doing great. "Can you look up when I'm talking to you?" she asks. "Thanks."

When she turns to write on the board, two boys in front of me slap palms and touch knuckles across the aisle. She passes around some handouts, and Michelle takes out her three-hole punch for anybody with three-ring binders.

In Spanish somebody's put up a new poster over the blackboard of an elephant on a beach ball. Over the elephant it says THE KEY TO LIFE IS BALANCE.

"What's on your *pack*?" the girl across from me asks.

Flake finds me in the hall before third period. "Go to the bathroom and wait for the bell before you come out," he goes. "Bring the whole duffel to the doors. I'll take care of the wedge. And wait till you see me at the double doors. Go in when I go in. Don't go in before I go in."

"Look at you two making your big plans," Tawanda says when she goes by.

In science the black girl who always takes her arms out of her sweater sleeves and sits there like a bundle hugs herself all class long. The bell rings after what seems like five minutes. My hands are numb. I blink three times to focus my eyes.

Everybody's heading in the same direction but me. On the way to the bathroom I pass one of the special-ed rooms. On the desk there's a stegosaur made of egg cartons. In the bathroom two kids are wrestling at the sink and I wait in a stall until they finally leave. The bell sounds for the start of fourth period.

I hear the pep band start up.

The hall's empty when I look out. The sound of kids finding a place to sit on the pullout bleachers is like a far-off rolling boom. One little kid runs past the stairs at the far end of the hall and skids when he tries to turn. My locker's right across from me. I cross to it and work the combination. I can hear the principal telling everyone to settle down. The second number slips so I start over. The next time the first number slips. The time after that everything goes right but the thing still doesn't open.

Michelle comes along while I'm yanking on the handle and kicking the door. "What're you doing?" she goes. "What's your combination?"

I tell her and she bends over and puts her face next to the lock and opens it. When she swings the door open I stop it halfway and thank her.

"You're gonna be later than I am," she goes, and then takes off.

When she's gone I wrestle the duffel out of the locker one end at a time. The principal starts in on the first part of his talk. I drag the duffel up onto my back and start for the gym. "And in JV footbaaaaall," the principal says, and the kids all cheer. It sounds like Flake's CD.

I dump the bag down before I look around the last corner. There's no one near the doors.

When was I supposed to load in the clip? I squat and root around for it, and then for the gun. I can't get the barrel clear of the bag. Finally I drop to my butt, stand the gun up, and ram the thing in. I remember another clip but it won't fit in my pocket. I grab the gun and run for the wall next to the doors. Flake hisses something so loud from the other doors that I can tell how pissed off he is even though I can't hear what he's saying. He leans out from the wall with his carbine.

I slap my back to the cinder block. My heartbeat's going in my ears. I hold the gun so the barrel's up and away from my face. I remember the safety and fumble it off.

When I look back at the other doors Flake's away from the wall and facing them. His expression is like he wishes he could scream in my ear. When he sees he's got my attention he grabs the handle and swings the door open and disappears.

I breathe in all the air I can and push away from the wall and grab the door handle myself. I pull the thing open.

Michelle's standing in front of me. She turns and looks at me and then looks at the gun.

The vice principal is next to the wall inside the door. I turn the barrel to him. He has a look like I found something strange in the hall and holds a hand out toward the stock.

Someone at the other door yells. Someone screams. Flake starts firing. My head recoils even at that distance and I put a hand to my ear. I forgot the earplugs again.

The sound freaks me out. The whole place ricochets with screaming. I see Weensie bumping down the bleachers head-first on his back. Another kid's knocked backward into a girl, and red confettis up his shirt.

Everybody who's not running away from Flake is running at him. One kid gets him around the neck and then falls over somebody underneath him and Flake puts the carbine in his belly and fires. He pulls the barrel away from that kid and keeps firing at everyone around him, the gun so low I can't see it anymore.

"Shoot your fucking *gun!*" he screams, and across from me a fat kid loses his footing trying to get off the bleachers and bowls down five or six girls. Flake fires off more rounds and there are other gunshots and he disappears. A security guard out in the middle of the floor is still aiming at him with a pistol and the vice principal knocks me flat and when I hit the ground the Kalashnikov goes off and wild thin trenches spike up out of the hardwood floor until my hand comes off the trigger. The concussion blows in both my ears, and over all the other noise there's a grinding, high-pitched sound like you hear at the bottom of a pool. It feels like my head is spiraling in on itself. An elbow cracks my ear and it sounds like a wooden block. I can't see if Flake's okay and somebody's got my legs. Some ninth-graders jump on the pile and the vice principal yells for them to get away but they don't listen. Kids are screaming and colliding trying to get through the doors and falling and climbing on the kids already down.

And I'm screaming louder no matter how deaf I am because I know where I'm headed, with cops and reporters and counselors and shrinks asking what I knew, everybody wanting to know what I was in on and what we wanted. The vice principal's shouting something in my ear and some kid's working on a headlock but I keep getting out of it. I'm crying and screaming Flake's name, which pisses off whoever's holding my arms, and they start punching my face to shut me up.

And weeks from now when they tell me how Flake died and actually *show* me on the tape from the security camera I'll see myself in the background, standing there pointing my gun and doing nothing with it. And Michelle will be like *He didn't shoot* and the vice principal will be like *He didn't shoot* and everybody will be like *Flake was the bad one, Flake fucked him up, Flake made him what he was.*

Because they *know* who Flake was. He took no shit and never lied to himself. *Good,* I think, *do it,* while they grind my head into the floor. Now I'm like everybody else—a liar—and nobody knows and nobody cares. Nothing about me is any good. Nothing I wanted to be is left. If I could get hold of the gun I'd turn it on myself. And sometime soon they'll be right: the danger *will* be past. My dad will say, standing in the hall one night when he thinks I'm asleep, "Maybe we're out of the fucking woods here." And we will be. No more woods. I'm a faggot. I'm a joke. I'm a blowup with nowhere to go, a dick who couldn't do one simple thing, a house burning down from the inside out.

A NOTE ON THE TYPE

This book was set in Caledonia, a Linotype face designed
by W. A. Dwiggins (1880–1956). It belongs to the family
of printing types called "modern face" by printers—a
term used to mark the change in style of the type letters
that occurred around 1800. Caledonia borders on the
general design of Scotch Roman but it is more freely
drawn than that letter.

Composed by Creative Graphics,
Allentown, Pennsylvania
Printed and bound by R. R. Donnelley & Sons,
Harrisonburg, Virginia
Designed by Virginia Tan